NICE GUYS STILL FINISH

The Ladies Who Brunch Book Five

HARLOW JAMES

Copyright © 2023 by Harlow James
All rights reserved.

No part of this book may be reproduced in any form or by any electronic or mechanical means, including information storage and retrieval systems, without written permission from the author, except for the use of brief quotations in a book review.

This is a work of fiction. Names, characters, businesses, places, events, locales, and incidents are either the products of the author's imagination or used in a fictitious manner. Any resemblance to actual persons, living or dead, or actual events is purely coincidental.

Special Edition Paperback ISBN: 9798369613009

Cover Designer: Abigail Davies, Pink Elephant Designs
Editor: Melissa Frey

This one is for my readers. Without your desire for Jeffrey's story, there wouldn't be one.
Thank you for loving him just as much as I do. And for loving this entire series.

And to the ladies who haven't found their man yet…
Marry the funny one. The nice one.
Show them that they can finish.
And I promise—they can make you finish too 😉

"There's a difference between a boy who kinda likes you, and a man who needs your soul next to his. Learn the difference."

Unknown Author

Contents

Prologue	1
Chapter 1	5
Chapter 2	21
Chapter 3	34
Chapter 4	43
Chapter 5	60
Chapter 6	74
Chapter 7	82
Chapter 8	97
Chapter 9	106
Chapter 10	124
Chapter 11	138
Chapter 12	151
Chapter 13	170
Chapter 14	181
Chapter 15	198
Chapter 16	206
Chapter 17	212
Acknowledgments	217
About the Author	219
More Books by Harlow James	221

Prologue

Jeffrey

Senior Year of High School

"Oh my God, Jeffrey! You always make me laugh!" Jessica snorts and then smacks me playfully.

And inside, I feel like a million bucks.

Make girls laugh. That's the key to getting them to like you, right?

"What can I say? I'm a funny guy. Who knows? Maybe I'll be a comedian one day."

She props her chin in her hand and smiles at me. "A *famous* comedian? Because then I could say, 'I know him! That's Jeffrey Davis. I went to high school with him.'"

"Or you could say, 'That's Jeffrey Davis. He's my boyfriend.'"

The laugh she lets out this time puts the last one to shame. "Oh, that's a good one!"

My stomach plummets, but I try so hard to keep a passive face. "Why's that so funny?" I ask instead, wondering if I've been reading this situation all wrong.

After months of crushing on Jessica from afar, I finally got the courage to talk to her during one of our classes together. After laying some groundwork, we realized we had a lot in common and worked well together. She even suggested that we team up on the project that's due at the end of the grading period.

And luckily, she was as amazing as I thought she would be—funny, smart, and gorgeous—although that was already a given. Every guy in our grade recognized how beautiful she was, and it was no secret that only a moron wouldn't jump at the chance to date her.

So here I was, months of laying the foundation of being her friend, offering a shoulder to cry on when she lost her volleyball games or got in a fight with her parents, and assuring her that her hair and outfits looked great every single day.

And now I was finally ready to ask her out.

But apparently the idea was hilarious.

"Because it's *you*, Jeffrey," she replied as if her answer just made sense. But I was still baffled.

"Okay . . ."

She punched my shoulder like a dude would do to one of his buddies. "You're my *friend*. One of my only guy friends, in fact. I love that I don't have to worry about you and I dating. It makes me feel like I can be myself around you."

Somebody come hand me a box of tissues because I legitimately think I might start crying. "But friends can turn into more sometimes . . ." I stab at one last glimmer of hope. Maybe she just hasn't envisioned the two of us together like that yet.

Because *I* have—every day for months. At night, when I masturbate until my dick might fall off. And even during class when we're working and I can't help but stare at her longingly.

"But that would ruin it. I don't want to destroy our friendship." Placing her hand over the top of mine, she says, "You're a *nice* guy, Jeffrey. The best. But I just don't think of you that way."

"Hey, Jessica!" one of the football players, Clayton Thompson, calls out across the cafeteria, catching Jessica's attention. "Come over here, sexy!"

She giggles and then turns back to me. "I've got to go. Rumor has it that Clayton is going to ask me to homecoming. He's so dreamy." With a kiss to my cheek, she stands. "I'll talk to you later, Jeff." And then I watch the girl of my dreams walk away toward another guy, a guy that I know for a fact won't treat her the way I could.

My heart feels like someone put it through a meat grinder. My stomach is churning to the point that I feel like I might get sick. But my confidence? That's what's truly shaken.

I must have read the entire situation wrong. The flirtatious banter and friendship we developed must have all been in my head. I swear she was feeling the same way I was.

But I guess I was mistaken.

Little did I know that this experience would become a broken record that continued to play all throughout college and even later into my adult life.

Because you know how the saying goes: Nice guys finish last.

And now I'm beginning to wonder if they even finish at all.

Chapter 1

Jeffrey

"Are you freaking kidding me?" I slap my palm to my face right after I feel moisture hit my skin. I pull my hand back to find a milky-white substance laced through my fingers. My other hand clutches the handle on the plastic bag I'm carrying, and I'm thankful that what I'm pretty sure is bird shit didn't hit its contents as well.

"What the fuck?" Looking up, I see a line of three seagulls perched on a telephone wire hanging over the path I'm walking on, pretending to mind their own business, but they aren't fooling me. "Did you seriously just shit on my head, you guys?"

A loud squawk echoes around me as their reply, but before I come back with my own retort, I consider two things: One, that I'd be arguing with birds at eight in the morning, and I don't need that kind of random negativity in my life today. And two, is having a bird poop on you lucky or unlucky?

Groaning, I lift the bottom of my shirt to wipe the bird shit from my face as I finish the walk up to the front gate of Greenlight Studios, a local television and movie production studio tucked up in the hills of San Diego, California. After the guard checks me in, I head to my right toward stage twenty-four, hoping that my sister at least has a spare shirt in her wardrobe that I can change into.

It's not every day that I get to visit Joselyn, no less on the set of her morning talk show. But today is her birthday, and I always make it a point to see her on that day no matter what. So we can celebrate together.

Yup, it's my birthday, too. That's how it works when you're a twin.

Bet you didn't see that little morsel about me coming, did you?

As soon as I get cleared at the door, the hustle and bustle of television production is all around me. People run past, yelling into microphones attached to their ears, giant lights and cameras are being maneuvered around the stage, and several people that look like they're in charge are huddled in front of the set, speaking to each other.

"Hey, Jeffrey." Melissa, one of the many employees here, greets me as I pass by. "Happy birthday!" It's well known around the studio that Joselyn has a twin, and she often talks about me on the show as well, so I feel like part celebrity when I'm here. And I have to admit, it's kind of fucking cool.

"Thanks." I shuffle down the hall farther until I come to the door of my sister's dressing room and hear her shouting on the other side. Well, that's not a good sign.

"I can't believe this!" Her angry voice echoes through the door just as I raise my hand to knock. "They can't just blindside me with this change and expect things to go smoothly."

A soft female voice replies, "Unfortunately, there's nothing in your contract that says you have a say in your cohost. I'm sorry, Jos."

"Ugh! This is just great. And did you see him and his smug smile?" I can imagine the narrow slit in her eyes as she speaks. "He has a punchable face, Ariel. I can't share a show with a man who has a punchable face!"

Ariel? Is my sister having a conversation with the Little Mermaid?

I decide now is just as good a time as any to knock and make my presence known.

"Come in!" My sister shouts as I turn the knob and see her pacing around her dressing room. Her long blonde hair is down around her shoulders, minus the few pieces on the top of her head that are tucked up in hot rollers. Her makeup is completely done, but she's walking around barefoot. She's wearing a beige pencil skirt with a white blouse, looking ever the morning talk show host that she portrays on television, but her frazzled state is impossible to miss.

"Jos! You okay?"

Her shoulders deflate as soon as she sees me, and she rushes toward me. She tries to launch herself into my arms, but I stop her just in time with a hand in the air.

"Might not want to hug me." I point to the bottom of my shirt where the bird shit resides. "A bird crapped on my head on the way in, and I don't want it to get on your outfit."

She giggles and then tears cloud her eyes as one falls slowly down her cheek. "That would only happen to you." Clutching her hands to her chest, she continues, "Oh my God, Jeffrey. It's so good to see you." Her body starts shaking like she's about to sob.

"Don't cry, sis. I missed you, too," I tease her.

Quieting, she swipes under her eye. "Sorry, it's just been a morning."

"I overheard a little bit outside. What's going on? You definitely shouldn't be crying on your birthday."

"Happy birthday to you, too," she replies, now smiling while reaching up to pinch my cheek.

I swat her hand away. "Enough of that. What's got you so flustered?"

She lets out a growl and begins to pace again. "The station has brought in a replacement for Tiffany, and let's just say, he's not making a great impression."

"Wait. Tiffany isn't coming back?"

"Nope!" She pops the p and lifts a finger in the air as she paces back and forth in a straight line, sliding right back into her rant. "I mean, I get it. She had a baby, but she said she was returning. Then last week, we got the news that she terminated her contract. For the past three years, it's been *Joselyn and Tiffany in the Morning* on channel thirteen. Our viewers have gotten used to seeing two female hosts as we discuss everything happening in San Diego and societal issues we deem important. And now, they've replaced her with this . . . this . . ."

"He's a dick," the girl standing in the corner chimes in, drawing my attention over to her. And fuck me sideways, why didn't I see her standing there before?

Barely over five feet tall, the short blonde stares at me as our eyes meet for the first time, her fiercely mocha-colored ones fixed on my blues. My heart races, and my eyes drift down to her pink lips, lips twisted in a purse that screams she's plotting a murder right now, and I'm not sure if it's for me or my sister's new colleague. She's wearing dark-wash jeans, a plain white t-shirt, and an olive-green army jacket, casual but also perhaps like she's trying to blend in. But now that I've seen her, I don't think I could ignore her presence if I tried.

As I continue to appreciate her beauty and forget that my sister is also in the room, the clipboard that she's clutching to her chest is screaming under the pressure she puts on it, and that makes me both terrified and intrigued by her passion, bringing me back to reality.

"A flaccid one or a hard one?" I ask the petite woman who arches a brow at me.

"Excuse me?"

"Well, I think that matters. A flaccid dick is worse than a hard one, you know? At least with an erection, there's promise of some pleasure at the end. But if he's soft, spongy, a little sad-looking, and hanging to the left . . . well, then that definitely makes him less appealing—a less appealing and unsatisfactory dick, if you will."

The girl shifts her eyes to my sister. "This is your brother?"

Joselyn comes up behind me, wrapping her arm around my shoulder even though I have a good five inches on her. "Yes. Jeffrey suffers from this condition called verbal diarrhea. The good news is that it's not contagious, but the bad news is that there is no cure."

"Charming," the woman replies, dropping her eyes down my body. And if I didn't know any better, I'd think she's checking me out. But since I still feel she looks a little bit murdery, I'd say she's searching for my weak spots or deciding where to plunge a knife into me first.

"I can be . . ."

My sister snorts. "Sure, Jeffrey. You must be selling your own kind of charm then." She moves across the room. "By the way, this is Ariel, my new assistant."

Aw, so no Little Mermaid. "Nice to meet you, Ariel." I reach out to shake her hand, and she actually reciprocates, but her pinched face seems to indicate that doing so physically hurts her.

"Pleasure," she replies sarcastically. I can't figure out if her annoyance is endearing or scary at this point.

Instead, I turn back to my sister. "What happened to Heather?"

"She got promoted."

"And so now she's stuck with me," Ariel interjects, straightening her spine and changing the subject, drawing my attention back to her. "Jos, I know it's your birthday, your brother is here"—

she darts her eyes over to me for a split second and then shifts back to my sister—"and you're in the middle of a meltdown, but we go to camera in thirty minutes, and Serena needs to finish your hair and probably touch up your makeup after the few tears you just shed."

Joselyn sighs. "Fine."

Ariel closes the distance between her and my sister, tossing her clipboard to the couch on the side of the room and then placing her hands on Joselyn's shoulders despite their considerable height difference. "Look, you're a professional. San Diego loves you. It doesn't matter who you have sitting in that chair next to you, you can do this job with your eyes closed. Just go out there, put on that brilliant fake smile, and show the network that *you* are what makes this show special, not the idiot of a man they chose to replace Tiffany, okay?"

"That's a pretty decent pep talk if I ever heard one," I say to my sister as Ariel glares at me, making my asshole pucker. *Jesus, this woman is wound tight.* "But she's right. You've got this. And after the show, we'll go to lunch like we planned." It's then I remember the bag I'm holding. "Plus, I brought you your favorite cupcakes from Grady's Bakery."

Jos's eyes light up. "The red velvet with cream cheese frosting?"

"Is there any other option?"

Taking a deep breath, my sister squares her shoulders. "You're right. Both of you. This ogre of a man has no idea who Joselyn Davis is." With renewed confidence, she marches to the door and leaves me and Ariel alone, staring at each other once we realize my sister is no longer here as a buffer.

Silence unnerves me. I can't handle it. It's why, most of the time, I let my mouth take over and just say whatever is on my mind to fill the void. More often than not, my mouth gets me in more trouble than I can handle, but my sister was right. I suffer from quote, unquote, "verbal diarrhea," and at this point in my life, I'm just as curious about what's going to come out of my mouth as everyone else is.

"So Ariel, huh? Your mom must have been obsessed with *The Little Mermaid* movie."

Rolling her eyes, Ariel reaches for her clipboard and flips one of the papers over before writing something down. "How original of you. Not like I've ever heard that one before. Although, most of the time, men just ask if I'm wearing a seashell bra under my clothing or blatantly point out that my hair isn't red."

That's actually pretty funny, but I don't dare say that out loud. "Nah, I always thought it was the tail that made her hot."

Ariel stops writing and stares up at me. "I'm sorry . . . what?"

"Her tail, you know . . . her fin?" I blow out a breath and then bite my lip. "Talk about hot. You just didn't know what that thing was capable of or what she was hiding underneath it. It was the mystery for me."

Ariel's lips are twisted up in disgust, and I abruptly realize I've taken this too far.

"But, uh . . . I like your name. Really. Very Disney princess but still suitable for you."

She lifts her hand up and closes her eyes. "Dear God, please stop talking."

"Noted."

"Your sister wasn't joking about your rambling, was she?"

"Her honesty is brutal at times but a noble trait, I think."

Shaking her head, she drops her clipboard on the couch again, marches over to a closet, opens the door, slides a few articles of clothing along the rod, and then rips a blue dress shirt off the hanger and tosses it at me. I nearly miss the catch but recover it nicely. "Change into that. I'm sure you don't want to continue walking around with bird shit on your shirt."

"Uh, not particularly." I reach for the hem of my shirt and start to pull it up, but Ariel nearly shrieks.

"What are you doing?"

"I'm changing."

"And wouldn't you like some privacy?"

"Why? It's just my shirt. It's not like you've never seen a naked man chest before, right? You've been to the beach or swimming in a pool at some point, correct?" I ask as I lift my shirt over my head, careful not to get more poop in my hair, and then toss it in a trash can in the corner. I don't really care about salvaging it at this point.

"Well, yeah, but . . ." She trails off mid-sentence as her eyes lock onto my torso, and damn, does it make me feel good.

I'm not the most muscular man on the face of the planet, but I do go to the gym four days a week and try to eat a balanced diet. I'm not looking to enter a body builder competition or get shredded because, honestly, I love food and beer. But I do like to feel comfortable in my skin and clothes, and the look that Ariel has on her face right now as she takes in my chest and arms makes me think that perhaps I'm in better shape than I thought.

The apples of her cheeks flush with a crimson hue that has my lips lifting in a smirk. "Like what you see?"

"Ugh, men." She twists around, presenting her back to me while reaching for her clipboard again. "Actually, I was looking to see if you had a third nipple or a wart with a hair growing out of it."

"Did you find anything?"

"Unfortunately not," she mumbles under her breath, but I catch it.

I finish the buttons on the front and then check my reflection in the mirror that spans one wall above a counter full of random feminine products. "All dressed now. You can look."

Wearily, she looks at me over her shoulder, relief in her eyes when she sees I was telling the truth. "Great. Now wash the bird shit out of your hair, and take your seat in the audience. I need to go check on Joselyn."

I reach up and spy in the mirror the remnants of the present the birds dropped on me this morning, and I groan as I realize I was trying to flirt with this woman with poop in my hair.

Were you flirting, Jeffrey? Or were you just trying to see if you could get this ice queen to crack a smile?

Before she leaves entirely, I call out to her. "Ariel?"

"Yeah?"

"Thanks for the shirt. And thanks for taking care of my sister."

Her face softens, and the slightest hint of a smile peeks through her lips. "You're welcome. And happy birthday, Jeffrey."

"Thanks, sweetheart."

"I'm not your sweetheart." She rolls her eyes one more time at me and then walks away, leaving me reeling over my interaction with one of the grumpiest women I've ever met. And then I make a mental note to bug Joselyn about her later.

I love women, but I don't have much luck when it comes to dating. My friends say that I don't know when to shut up, which is true. My sister says I just haven't found the right person yet, which could also be true. And women? Well, their feedback is all over the place. Some say I don't know how to be serious, some want a man who's taller or more muscular, some want the asshole which just isn't me, and some say that I feel more like a friend to them than a romantic partner, which stings. I mean, as a man, you just can't hear that enough. *I just think it's better that we're friends.*

I've been friend-zoned so many damn times that I've lost count.

So needless to say, it's been a while since I've put myself out there. All of my friends are married or engaged by now, including Damien, my best friend and colleague. Hell, he actually has a one-year-old daughter now and is loving life as a dad. But me? I feel like I'm behind in a race that everyone else has already finished. And I know that life isn't a race, but it's difficult to see others get the girl—get the life you wanted—and feel as if it may never happen for you.

I haven't given up hope, though, and after my little run-in with Ariel, perhaps there's a spark between us I should explore further.

I could have been reading our entire interaction incorrectly, which I do more often than not. But if I didn't know any better, I would think the woman was attracted to me, and I sure as hell know I'm attracted to her. Even the predominant scowl on her face was sexy, and that's saying something.

So that's when I decide that I want to know more about the Little Mermaid masquerading as Elsa. And I want to know more about her soon.

∽

"Today wasn't that bad," I say as I wince at my sister sitting across from me in the booth on our lunch date.

"Jeffrey, the man argued with me about every point I was trying to make."

"That makes for good television! Different viewpoints, right?" I say, but I'm thinking back at how red Joselyn's face was turning on camera, and I know her new cohost was just trying to get a rise out of her.

See? Other guys can be assholes, and women throw themselves at their feet, but I try to make them laugh or show them I care, and I get friend-zoned. I just don't get it.

"This isn't going to work. I can't do this. I can't sit across from Hunter five days a week and pretend that I'm interested in what he has to say. I might end up jamming a pen in his eye on national television and then be arrested for attempted murder."

"Don't do that. You hate jumpsuits of any kind, and I don't want to have to visit you in prison." I shudder. "Just the thought has me wanting to pee myself."

"Dear Lord, please don't do that."

I reach across the table to grab her hand, our plates pushed to the side now that we've finished eating. "It's gonna be okay. Perhaps the studio executives will realize that you and Hunter don't mix, and they'll find someone else?"

Joselyn sighs. "I don't see that happening. Part of the reason he was considered is because of who his brother is."

"Yeah, that does present a problem."

Hunter Palomar, my sister's new colleague, just so happens to be one of Hayden Palomar's older brothers. Hayden plays for the Los Angeles Bolts as their first-string running back, and he's also one of my closest friends. I met him through Maddox Taylor, the husband of one of Charlotte's—Damien's wife—best friends. It's an intricate web, but Hayden and I immediately hit it off and formed a bromance. My sister possibly murdering his brother might change that.

I'll have to talk to Hayden about it the next time I see him. "Well, maybe Hayden can speak with him? Get him to lay off?"

Jos glares at me. "Don't you dare get him involved. If Hayden goes back and tells Hunter anything you said that I said, he could use it against me." She stares off toward the side of the restaurant. "No, this has to be calculated. I need to get him to quit or, at the very least, make him realize that I'm not backing down from him. This is *my* show. He's the new guy. He needs to adhere to the hierarchy already present, even if I am a woman."

I reach up to give her a high five, which she reciprocates, thank God. There's nothing worse than when someone leaves you hanging in that situation. "That's right, Jos. Show him who's boss. I think this will all work out."

"I hope so."

"Now, not to change the subject on you, but what's the deal with Ariel?"

My sister smirks across the table at me, relaxing now in her side of the booth. "You want to know about Ariel?"

I draw circles on the table in front of me, avoiding her eyes. "I mean, nothing in particular. Just . . . curious."

Joselyn slams her hand on top of mine so I stop doodling, forcing my eyes to hers. "What happened when I left my dressing room today?"

"Nothing much." I exhale and lean back in my seat this time. "She gave me this shirt to change into, I asked her about her name—"

Jos snorts. "Oh, I'm sure she loved that."

"Yeah, not so much. But I don't know . . . there's something about her that intrigues me. I was trying my darndest to make her smile, but she's a tough nut to crack."

My sister smiles softly. "Yeah, she is, but she really is a genuine person. Truth be told, I don't know too much about her. She's kind of private, but she's a hard worker, very independent, dependable, loyal . . . she's got a good soul, but you can tell she's not quick to let people in."

"That sucks." I wonder who hurt her. Every woman always has one man who changes her forever, and part of me wishes I could castrate each and every one of them.

"Yeah, but I could see you two together." She tilts her head to the side as she studies me. "I feel like you would be good for her."

"I've heard that before."

"I'm serious, Jeffrey. She's sort of quiet and a little intense, and you're . . ."

"Not?"

She laughs. "Yeah. You guys could be a classic case of opposites attract, though. Do you want me to talk to her?"

I shrug. "I mean, maybe just feel her out? I don't want to get invested if she's not even looking for something right now. I've been down that road, and it's not fun."

"I know, Jeff, but you're going to find someone. I just know it."

"You, too, Jos."

She sighs and then clears her throat. My sister struggles in the romance department just as much as I do. "Well, it's really hard to date when you're in the public eye. You have no idea who's genuine and who's not, who wants something from you and who's just looking to say they hooked up with someone famous, even though I'm on like the C-list of celebrities."

"Hey, C's get degrees. That's the saying, right?"

She chuckles. "That has absolutely nothing to do with what we're talking about."

"I know, but it just sounded good at the time."

Jos reaches for my hand again. "I'm so glad we got to see each other today. We need to make it happen more often, Jeff."

"I know. Life is just crazy. Work is insane for both of us, and now that Mom and Dad are traveling more, we aren't having dinners with them as much."

"I know. I'm happy for them, but it's like they forgot about us."

"We're in our thirties now, but I still want Mom's cooking once in a while, you know?"

"Absolutely."

Laughing at each other, we stand and grab our to-go boxes, heading back out to our cars to return to our days. I took the day off of work, but I do want to hit the gym before I meet up with Damien and the guys for beers.

"Well, I'll call you later this week then? Maybe we can do dinner?"

"Sounds good, sis. I love you."

She pushes up on her toes and plants a kiss on my cheek "I love you, too, bro. Happy birthday."

"Same to you."

Chapter 2

Jeffrey

"I never realized how many euphemisms there are for penis." I drop the book in my lap and stare out across the group of men sitting in a circle around me.

"Really?" Hayden turns so our eyes meet.

"For sure. Cock, dick, schlong, erection, hardness, length, junior—"

"Lightsaber," he interjects.

"You call yours a lightsaber?"

He nods. "Absolutely. It can be used for good or evil and can light up any woman's world." He bounces his eyebrows up and down as the rest of our group cackles.

It's Tuesday night, which means it's our monthly book club meeting. Now, I know what you're thinking. It's not that often you hear about a book club where the members are only men, and that's because this isn't just any old book club. No, the Smartest Men Alive (our coined name because it's true) was created by Hayden Palomar to help educate men in the realm of romance and, in turn, women. Reading romance books is one of the most underrated ways to understand what women want from men. These books are like guides into their brains and desires. So guess what we read exclusively? Yup, you guessed it—romance.

"You see, I think variety is key," John, another member of our group, chimes in. "I feel like there are only so many times I can read the word 'cock' before I grow tired of it."

"Yeah, but what if the woman is saying it? Like, think about real life . . . if I'm having sex with a woman, and she keeps talking about my cock while using that word, I don't think I'd mind hearing it repeatedly," Hayden counters.

"But what if she called it a lightsaber?" Shifting in my seat, I look my friend dead in the eye. And then, in as feminine a voice as I can muster, I say, "'Oh, baby. Slide your lightsaber into my pussy.'" The guys lose all decorum as their laughter carries throughout the entire bookstore.

Hayden hums in thought. "I see your point."

"I think there are just some things you can get away with in books but not real life. Or at least, it's hotter when you're reading it than if it happened in reality."

"Like choking," Kellan chimes in. "I wouldn't dare choke a woman in real life unless she asked for it. But when we polled listeners on the podcast, an overwhelming majority of women said they loved reading about it. Romance helps bridge the gap between reality and fantasy and at least gives women the courage to ask for what they want in bed."

Kellan joins Hayden as a cohost of the romance podcast that Hayden started, specializing in book reviews from the male perspective. He does interviews with the authors sometimes—which is always a fun experience—takes questions from the listeners, and brings on some of us knuckleheads from time to time as guests to mix it up.

Let's just say I'm a little bit of a fan favorite for obvious reasons: my blatant honesty and lack of control over my mouth and what comes out of it.

"So perhaps we need to poll the listeners about their favorite euphemism for penis on the next podcast and open up a discussion about that?" Hayden suggests.

Nodding, I say, "I am definitely curious about what the fan favorite will be."

"Dear Lord . . . what the hell did I just walk in on?"

Spinning in my seat so fast that I nearly fall out of my chair, I lock onto the petite blonde who's been on my mind for the past five days. Ariel's brow is scrunched up so tight that she looks like she's trying to solve a calculus problem in her head. But depending on how long she's been listening to our discussion, I'm sure that puzzled look is due to the number of questions going through her mind at the moment.

"Ariel!" I exclaim, twisting my entire body around in my chair. "What a surprise!"

"Jeffrey, I know we just met, but I'm genuinely concerned about the conversation I just eavesdropped on."

"Care to add to it?" Kellan suggests as the rest of the men give her their attention now.

"You know this woman, Jeffrey?" Hayden asks.

My eyes flicker in his direction. "I mean, she works with my sister . . . and your brother now, I guess."

Ariel unfolds her brow and then shoots a glare in Hayden's direction. "You're Hunter's brother?"

"The one and only." He stands from his seat, stretching out his hand. "Hayden Palomar. Nice to meet you."

Ariel eyes him skeptically before shaking his hand. "At least you have better manners than your brother." Hayden laughs. "Ariel Logan."

"Is my brother rubbing everyone the wrong way already?" Hayden jokes.

"You sound like that's what you expect to hear," she counters.

"I swear, he's not a bad guy. He just . . . doesn't always paint himself in the best light."

"That's the understatement of the year," Ariel replies before directing her attention back to me. "So does Joselyn know that you sit around talking about penises with other men on a Tuesday night?"

The group of men behind me snicker, and my lips slide into a wide smile that I've been told is rather charming. "Yes, she does, actually."

"Interesting. So, what is this?" She waves her hands toward us. "The He-Man Woman Hater's Club?"

Hayden steps up. "No, it's the Smartest Men Alive Book Club, to be exact. We read romance novels to gain insight into the wants and desires of women."

Ariel breaks out into obnoxious laughter, holding her stomach. But then she realizes we're all staring at her, serious as a heart attack. "Oh. That wasn't a joke?"

Hayden smirks at her. "No, babe. It wasn't."

Her eyes narrow at him again. "I'm not your *babe*."

Huh. Good to know I'm not the only one who's having a tough time breaking through her shell.

Before she claws his eyes out, I decide to step up. "Hey, since you're here, why don't you let me buy you a coffee?"

She bounces her gaze back and forth between me and Hayden before she sighs and relents. "A coffee would be great, actually."

As she turns and heads toward the café on the other side of the bookstore, I turn back around to check in on the guys. "I'll be right back."

"Be careful with that one," Kellan declares. "She might slit your throat when you're not looking."

"I think I'll be okay," I say, even though I haven't the faintest clue if that's true. But hell, what are the odds that I run into her in the middle of our book club meeting? And also, if I don't take advantage of the opportunity with her now, I'll kick myself later.

She's been on my mind for days—those pouty pink lips, the wrinkle between her brows when she's scowling at me and pretty much anyone else, her quick wit and sarcasm, they're all things that make her more interesting to me. She's not like other girls, and truth be told, I don't want someone easy to win over, amendable or complacent. I want to earn the woman who chooses me. I don't want something ordinary, I want something extraordinary. And who knows if I'll find that with Ariel, but I'll kick myself if I don't try to find out.

Searching the store, I see the back of Ariel's striking blonde hair near the counter of the café where she's scouring the menu, deciding on what to order. Taking a deep breath of courage, I march over to where she stands, lining up my body with hers so our shoulders would meet if there weren't such a considerable height difference between us.

"So, what's your poison?"

She lets out a heavy sigh. "I'm trying to decide if I should get coffee and risk being up until two in the morning or settle for decaffeinated tea instead."

"They have a pomegranate green tea that's caffeine free—my buddy gets it all the time. He says it's really good."

"Your romance-reading friends drink tea?"

"No, I was talking about my best friend and coworker, actually. He doesn't drink coffee at all, just tea . . . so I trust his judgment."

Blinking, she turns back to the menu. "Your resource sounds reputable, so I'll try it."

"Perfect. And I'll take that, too," I say, reaching for the book in her hands so I can pay for it.

"Jeffrey, I don't need you to buy my book."

"I know. I want to." Taking a page from the advice of the podcast listeners, I walk up to the counter and order two teas for us, a few of their shortbread cookies, and pay for Ariel's book before motioning for her to follow me to the other end of the counter to wait for our order.

"That was unnecessary," she mutters as she takes the book from my hands.

"A simple 'thank you' would suffice. I mean, isn't it a woman's dream for a man to buy their book for them in the bookstore?"

She gives me that perplexed look again. "Did you get that from your romance novels?"

"In fact, I did," I say proudly.

She sighs heavily again. "Thank you," she mumbles. "That was very nice of you, even if it wasn't necessary."

I playfully bump her shoulder. "That sounded like it physically hurt you to say."

A snort leaves her lips, and the sound may as well have been someone handing me a gold medal. "It did. I'm sorry, I'm just not used to men being nice for no reason. But I'm not sure if most women would find that romantic, particularly the independent, stubborn ones like myself who can pay for their own things." And then her eyes widen. "Oh God. Now you think I'm going to sleep with you, don't you?"

"What? No!" My heart starts racing. "Seriously, Ariel . . . I was just trying to be nice."

Ariel tips her head back as she laughs. "Oh, man. Your face was priceless."

"Did you . . . did you just crack a joke?"

Her smile falls. "Yes, Jeffrey. I can be funny, too, you know."

The barista calls out our order at that moment, and I'm grateful for the break in our conversation since my head spins faster the longer our interaction goes on. Ariel steps up to the counter to retrieve our drinks and cookies, and I motion for us to take a seat at one of the tables, knowing I won't be going back to the book club just yet. Thankfully, Ariel follows my lead.

"So, are you a big reader?"

Ariel looks down at the book, which has a colorful cover that looks like it could contain a romance. The illustrated art on the front gives nothing away, though—it's hard to tell the genre from the cover these days. Fortunately, I've read the book, so I'm aware of its contents. "Normally, no. But I'm all for trying new things, and a friend of mine recommended this story to get me out of my funk."

"Well, it's a good book. Probably a two on the chili pepper rating scale for spice, but I think you might like it, especially if you haven't enjoyed a spicy book recently."

Her mouth drops open. "You've read this one?"

I smile proudly and take a sip of my tea. "Yup."

"Who the hell are you?"

I reach across the table and offer her my hand. "My name is Jeffrey Davis. I'm Joselyn Davis's brother, whom you know. I work in advertising, read romance novels in my spare time, and buy books for girls I think are beautiful and intriguing."

The corner of her mouth lifts as well as one of her eyebrows.

"So you're saying I'm not the first woman you've bought a book for?"

"Shit." I run a hand through my hair, my stomach knotting. "No, you are. I didn't mean for it to come out that way . . ."

She giggles. "It's okay, Jeffrey." Studying me intently, she says, "You're really bad at this flirting thing, aren't you?"

"Is that what you think?"

"Maybe." She tilts her head at me. "I don't know. I'm still deciding."

"Well, what if I took you out on a date so you can make an official decision?"

Her face instantly falls, and then she's staring at the cardboard cup in her hands. "I don't think that's a good idea."

"Why not?"

She lifts her eyes to me again. "I work with your sister, for one."

"So? I don't think Joselyn would mind . . ."

"And two?" She winces. "I just don't think you're my type."

Like someone popped my balloon right in front of me, my hope deflates. "Can't hear that enough."

"Look, it's not you, it's—"

"Please, for the love of God, don't say 'it's me.'" Sighing, I mutter, "I get it. Don't worry. No hard feelings." But then something in my chest sparks, a flame of perseverance that I haven't felt in ages. And when an idea forms in my brain, I just decide to run with it. For once in my life, I don't want to take no for an answer from this girl. And not in an I-can't-accept-that-she-isn't-into-me kind of way, because my gut is telling me that she is. Maybe she just needs a little push, and it won't hurt for me to push myself as well.

"I'm used to this, anyway. Women just aren't sure what to do with me."

"Well, you are a lot to handle."

I chuckle. "Oh, honey, you don't know the half of it."

She glares at me again. "I'm not your honey."

Laughing, I take a sip of my tea. "It's just as well. Seems even the romance novels I'm reading aren't helping me in the dating arena."

"Well, I appreciate the effort, but women can't be understood by some cookie cutter formula. We're intricate beings. We're unique. What works for some doesn't work for others."

"I know . . . and it's exhausting trying to figure it all out."

"But we do like a lot of the same things from men."

My brows shoot up. "Like what?"

"Well, um . . ." Her eyes dart around the area, looking anywhere but at me. "Loyalty, consistency, and honesty for starters. But those are bare minimum expectations, I feel."

And then I smack the table, pretending I just came up with a brilliant idea, which I did—but about three minutes ago. "What if *you* helped me?"

Her mouth falls open. "What are you talking about?"

"What if you helped me figure out what I'm doing wrong, Ariel?"

"Uh . . ."

"Like a relationship tutor or coach. You're honest, and I need that. I need to know if what I'm doing is rubbing women the wrong way." I reach forward and grab her hand, jutting out my bottom lip. "Please . . . I could really use the help. Obviously, you're not attracted to me, so it's perfect. You'll help me find the woman of my dreams, and I'll help you . . ."

Her brow lifts when I don't continue. "Help me what?"

"Uh . . ." *Shit, Jeffrey. You didn't think this all the way through, like normal.*

She releases her hands from mine, crossing her arms over her chest. "What exactly do I need help with?"

"Well, you did say you were in a funk?" *Yeah, let's go with that.* "Maybe I can help you out with that? Take you out, buy you dinner, show you that the world isn't some dark place out to get you—"

"Is that what you think of me?"

"No offense, but you're not exactly easygoing or super friendly at first. Hell, the fact that you played a joke on me earlier almost gave me a heart attack."

Her smile threatens to peek through, but she covers it up quickly. "I just hate bullshit. I hate fake people. I don't want to spend time getting to know someone when inevitably they'll leave or lie—" She slams her mouth shut before she can utter another word, as if she just realized what she said, and reaches for one of the shortbread cookies instead.

Interesting. The woman has clearly been hurt, just as I thought. And if I want to prove to her that I'm worth taking a shot on, I have to show her that I'm not going to hurt her—at least, not intentionally.

"What's the risk of getting to know me, though, if I'm just some dorky guy who's hopeless with dating? I mean, it's not like you're going to fall for me."

I'm gonna make you fall for me so damn hard, Ariel who is not the Little Mermaid, that you won't know what happened until it's too late.

"I don't know . . ." She hesitates, taking a bite of her cookie and closing her eyes as she chews. "Oh my God, that's good."

I lean forward in my chair. "Those cookies are Joselyn's favorite. She got me hooked on them, so I feel it's necessary to curse everyone else with the addiction as well."

"That's not very nice."

"Yeah, but that's the problem. I'm always the nice guy." Dropping my eyes, I stare down at the table, not wanting to break apart in front of her, but hoping my melancholy grants me a little bit of sympathy from her. "Look, Ariel. Do me a favor. Don't answer me right now. Just think about it, okay? Take a few days, think about how much you'd be helping out a friend—"

"You're not my friend."

I lift my eyes to hers again. "Yeah, but Joselyn is, and she wants me to be happy and find someone just as much as I want that for her. And if you won't date me for real, why can't we be friends? You'd be helping us both." *Come on, don't shut this down already, before you've considered it . . .*

Rolling her eyes, she plops the last bite of cookie in her mouth, finishes chewing, and then says, "Okay. I'll think about it."

"Yes. Thank you!" I reach for her hand again, rubbing my thumb across the top of it. And the sparks I feel when I touch her—that can't just be one-sided.

As if I've burned her, she pulls her hand away from me and launches herself out of her seat, grabbing her book and tea from the table. "Fine. Yeah. I'll, uh . . . I'll get in contact with you."

Then she's gone, but the smile on my face is back. And so is the inkling that maybe putting in the effort with this woman will be worth it this time.

Chapter 3

Ariel

"I think you should go with the red dress. Red is a power color. It screams 'don't fuck with me.'" Holding the dress up by the hanger, I watch Joselyn's eyes bounce back and forth between my choice and a sky-blue pantsuit that I know would also look phenomenal on her. But based on the tension between her and Hunter for the past three days, I think she needs a small boost of confidence in the form of her attire.

"You're right. Red it is."

I hand her the dress and then turn my back to put the pantsuit on the rack as she changes. "So, what did he do this time?"

"The jerk took the last blueberry muffin, Ariel. Right as I was reaching for it. It was like watching his hand move in slow motion. He swooped in, took my last little speck of joy that I look forward to each morning, and then smirked like the asshole he is as he took a bite from it right in front of me."

Folding my lips in to hide my smile, I say, "Maybe he doesn't know that those are your favorite."

"Oh no, he does. One of the assistants told him: 'Make sure you leave one for Joselyn or she'll be cranky,'" she mocks in a slightly deeper voice. "First of all, I want to know when people assumed that an item of food would dictate my mood. And second, as soon as he obtained that information, he used it against me. He just declared war as far as I'm concerned."

Spinning to face her, I reply, "Over a blueberry muffin?"

Joselyn throws her hands in the air. "It's not about the muffin! It's about what the muffin represents!"

"Okay. Okay. Calm down." I walk over to her, bringing her hands back down to her sides. "Take a deep breath." Inhaling with her, I guide her through a couple of deep, soothing breaths while holding her hands before I speak again. "I think we've established the guy is a dick, Jos. So you need to decide if you're going to stoop down to his level or kill him with kindness."

"Normally, I'm all about taking the high road, but I don't think I can do it this time. I keep trying to remind myself of what Michelle Obama says: 'When they go low, you go high.' But all I want to do is go so low that I punch him in the balls, Ariel. This isn't good." Her gaze drifts to the side of the room as she bites her lip, her brow pinching as well.

"Why?"

Closing her eyes, she lets out the longest sigh-and-groan combination. "I had a dream about him the other night."

My eyebrows shoot up as my lips follow. "Really? What kind of dream?"

She pops one eye open to glare at me. "What kind of dream do you think?"

Giggling, I say, "Okay. So you had a dirty dream about him . . ." I let her hands go as she spins and starts to pace, a common occurrence for her, I've discovered. I think it's part of how she processes things, and I've learned to just let her do her thing.

"Now all I see when I look at him is the man who gave me an orgasm in my sleep."

"Must have been a good dream."

"You don't know the half of it," she mutters. "It's been so damn long since I've felt so out of control with my body around a man, Ariel. Just his presence makes my internal temperature rise. I want to smack his face while simultaneously sitting on it."

Chuckling, I say, "Girl, you're preaching to the choir. I've lost count of how long it's been since I've had sex." I busy myself with tidying up her dressing room so I don't have to look in her eyes as she processes our shared predicament.

"Well, that reminds me. I wanted to ask you something."

Twisting to face her again, I draw in a breath. "What?"

"You know my brother, Jeffrey?"

Oh, I know your brother, all right—too many details about him that make him one of the most perplexing men I've ever met, if I'm being honest. And I also know that the man is annoyingly charming and a little bit of a hot mess but entertaining nonetheless.

"Yeah . . ."

"He was asking about you while we were at lunch on my birthday."

"And?"

"Well, how would you feel about going out with him?"

How would I feel? If that isn't the exact question I've been asking myself for the past forty-eight hours since I ran into him at the bookstore the other night. Talk about a fluke, a chance encounter to the hundredth degree.

The last person I anticipated crossing paths with was him—and certainly not finding him participating in a book club with other men who read romance novels. My mind is still trying to wrap itself around that idea.

But then he bought me a tea, those shortbread cookies that I also haven't been able to stop thinking about, and my book. *He bought me a book.* My heart lurched a bit at that gesture, but I'll be damned if I admitted that. He was right. It is a dream for any avid reader, woman or not, to have someone buy a book for them. In fact, I think that gesture could be marketed as its very own love language.

But I can't tell Joselyn this. I can't admit that the man has my head spinning because that means admitting that I feel out of control and vulnerable, and that's not a place I like to be with men.

I've been burned one too many times.

First by my own father. Then by my ex. Lies, secrets, and

shades being pulled over my eyes twice was enough for me to make sure that I never put myself in a position to be blindsided by a man ever again.

But I don't want to admit that piece of information either, so instead, I deflect. "Uh, I don't date."

"What? Why?"

"Because men are pigs. I mean, look at Hunter, for example. You can't deny that."

"Yeah, but not all men are like Hunter."

"No, but a lot are, and I'd rather not take my chances. I make sure they know I'm not interested very early on."

Joselyn chuckles. "Clearly your don't-fucking-talk-to-me look is working well for you, then?"

"Yes, it is. If I can make a grown man piss in his pants, I know I'm giving off the right vibes."

"You made a man pee himself?"

"Yes, I did," I state proudly. "He was hitting on me—not in an endearing way, I might add—and I put him in his place so fast that he didn't even know what hit him."

Smirking and crossing her arms over her chest, she says, "Well, I hate to say this and sound cliché, but my brother is *not* most men."

I snort. "Yeah, I kind of gathered that." He's like a little puppy that wants to play fetch and keeps bringing you back everything but the ball you threw, but he's so damn cute that you can't help but just pat his head and keep praising him for trying.

"He's really very sweet and funny, incessant rambling aside."

Planting my hands on my hips, I shake my head in amusement. "I couldn't get over the shit that came out of his mouth, Jos. Who the hell talks about flaccid dicks with a stranger?"

"Jeffrey does." She shrugs, still smiling. "But at least you know he'll always keep you laughing, right? And there's never a dull moment when he's near."

Tilting my head from side to side, I say, "Look, I appreciate the offer. But he already asked me out, and I turned him down."

"Really? When?"

"I ran into him Tuesday night at Valor Books."

She nods in understanding. "Ah. Was he with his book club?"

"Yes. And that's another thing . . . does he really think that reading those books is going to help him with women?"

She full-on laughs. "I guess. I learned a long time ago not to argue with him too much about what he believes, especially when it comes to women. My brother hasn't had the best dating luck, but he's never given up hope that he'll find the right person one day. You can't knock him for being persistent and trying to better himself. That's actually pretty admirable, if you think about it."

"Yeah, I guess . . ."

"I just know that he has a lot to offer the right person, and I don't know . . ." She drops her eyes down and back up my body before landing on my face again. "I could see you two together."

Huffing out a laugh, I turn away from her again. "Are you sure you haven't been hitting the liquor this morning?"

"Ariel . . ." The sound of endearment in her voice has me

turning toward her again, afraid of what she might say. "What's the worst that could happen if you give him a chance?"

He could break my heart when it's barely been staying taped together for the past two years.

"I think we'd be better off as friends," I say instead. "I'm not looking for a relationship right now, anyway. I don't want to lead him on."

She sighs in defeat. "Well, I can't fault you for that. But he won't be single forever. Some lucky girl is gonna snatch him up one day and know how fortunate she is to have found him."

Yeah, but that won't be me.

She walks over to her desk, scribbles something on a Post-it note, and then hands it to me. "But just in case you change your mind, here's his number."

Taking the Post-it from her, I stare at the digits and momentarily debate telling her about his proposition from the other night, the one where he asked me to coach him on dating, but I decide against it. One, I haven't made up my mind completely about whether I'm going to do it or not. And two, I don't want to involve Joselyn if nothing transpires there. It's easier just to take this one day at a time right now, focusing on making a decision about donating my time to help him or not.

Do I want to help him find a girl who isn't me?

Yes, because you don't want him, remember, Ariel?

Please. You're lying to yourself right now. You're curious about the man, but you just can't admit it yet.

My stomach is twisted in knots at my ideas about how this

could go. Would he want me to watch him go on dates, stake out at a table nearby so I can give pointers later? Would I have to watch him kiss other girls? Would he come to me for advice about sex?

You haven't had sex in so long they may have changed how it's done, Ariel, so don't get too cocky.

"Ariel?" Joselyn's voice pulls me from my thoughts.

"Yeah?"

"I need to get to the set. How do I look?"

I realize she's standing in front of me in the red dress that highlights every single one of her curves. Her makeup and hair look flawless but not overdone, and she's smiling at her reflection in the mirror.

"Hunter's jaw is gonna hit the floor when he sees you."

She fluffs her hair and pushes up her boobs in her dress, highlighting her cleavage. "Good. Let him drool. Let him see what he'll never have."

"Only in your dreams, right?" I tease her.

She lets out a groan and then glares at me over her shoulder as she makes her way to the door. "That stays between us, Ariel. Don't make me start a war with you, too."

Laughing, I pump my fist in the air. "Girl power, Jos. I've got your back."

She smiles. "Thanks. And I've got yours, too. Thanks for being a friend." And then she leaves as I stand there feeling something funny take over my chest.

Friendship. It's not every day that people come into your life who are genuine and honest. And that's exactly who Joselyn is. She may be a little high-strung, but she's obviously going through something very stressful right now.

But you know who isn't high-strung? Her brother.

"Ugh," I groan out loud to myself as my thoughts drift back to Jeffrey again. And that's when I decide—if Joselyn is my friend, then Jeffrey can be mine, too. And maybe if I spend time with him as a friend, my head and heart will start to agree on if I want more from him.

I'm not choosing any direction at the moment, but my curiosity is winning, and part of me just wants to see what happens. I want to know more about this man who talks about flaccid dicks and buys me books. I want to know if behind his silliness is a man who can make my toes curl in the bedroom. And if he's not that man for me, then at least I can help him be that man for another woman.

I'm doing society a favor. Think of it as community service, if you will. If Jeffrey is going to date some other woman, the least I can do is make sure he's nothing like my ex, or my dad, or any other short-dicked man who doesn't understand the concepts of honesty, loyalty, and unconditional love. I can make sure he has manners, maybe help him control his zany outbursts a little, and make the world a better place for all womankind.

So it's settled.

Add "dating coach" to my resume because I guess I just accepted my first client.

Chapter 4

Ariel

"Let me guess . . . you ordered the pomegranate green tea?"

Spinning around in my chair, I find Jeffrey towering over me, wearing his signature grin that highlights the dimples in his cheeks, dimples I forgot about until I saw him just now.

I shake my cup full of ice since I ordered it cold this time. "What can I say? You made me a convert."

"No more coffee, then?" he asks as he takes a seat across from me at the same table we sat at before. It's Friday night, and unlike most people our age, we're meeting at the coffee shop in the bookstore instead of a bar or a swanky restaurant. When I called Jeffrey to tell him I reached a decision about his proposition, I thought meeting in a familiar setting would be best.

"Oh no. I'm a caffeine-in-the-morning girl for sure, but this tea definitely hits the spot at night."

He nods in agreement. "Good to know." Then he rubs his hands together in excitement. "So, Ariel, is this meeting going to make the smile on my face grow or turn upside down into a frown? Because I have to say that when I got your message, I squealed like a little girl in my office. Damien came running in to make sure I was okay."

"Jesus," I mutter, wondering for the hundredth time what I've gotten myself into. "And what did you tell him?"

"That the Little Mermaid finally called me back. I'm pretty sure he thought I was high until I explained everything to him." He winks, but all I can do is let out a low growl.

"No more Little Mermaid jokes, all right? Would you do that with a girl you were seriously trying to date?"

Recognition dawns on his face. "Well, that depends. Are you saying you're going to help me after all?"

With a purse of my lips, I pause for dramatic effect. "If we do this, you need to listen to what I say, understand?"

Glee spreads across his lips. "Don't worry, Ariel. I'll be listening to every damn word that comes out of those pouty pink lips."

The grate of his voice as he says those words has me clenching my thighs together.

No, that's not good. This is going to get complicated very quickly if you can't keep your libido in check, Ariel. Remember, you're helping out a friend. He might be interesting, but you need to keep your feelings under lock and key for now. There's no use getting your hopes up that he could prove you wrong.

Of course, no man yet has done that, so the odds are very low.

I clear my throat to get us back on track. "Fine. Then yes, Jeffrey, I agree to help you."

He jumps from his seat, fist-pumping the air. "Hell, yeah!" People around us all stare as I slouch down in my chair.

"For crying out loud, sit down," I grate out, hiding behind my hair. "The last thing a woman wants is to be embarrassed by her date."

His face falls as his ass follows, plopping back down into his chair. "I'm embarrassing?"

Shit. "Um, no. Not completely. I guess that word wasn't the right choice. It's just that . . ."

Much to my surprise, he starts laughing. "Don't worry, Ariel. That wouldn't be the first time I've heard that. I'm used to it by now, but I can't apologize for who I am." He shrugs but still has the biggest smile on his face.

"You're just a lot to handle, Jeffrey. You need to ease into how loud, exuberant, and animated you can be. It's not a bad thing, believe me. But that's something that you should save for when you've established a connection with a woman."

"But I thought we already have that?" he asks genuinely.

"We do, but you also need to treat our interactions as if they are dates. I think it will benefit you instead of trying to flip a switch back and forth every time."

He nods and then sits up straighter. "Okay, boss. I can do that."

He reaches out his hand for me. "Ariel, I want to thank you for agreeing to help me. Your time and dedication mean a lot, and I promise to be the best student I can be."

My brow furrows. "Okay, now you're acting kinda stiff."

He throws his hands in the air. "What do you want from me, woman?"

"Just be yourself," I toss back, throwing my own hands up.

"I was! That reaction was one hundred percent me!"

"Ugh! We're getting off track." Dropping my hands, I sit back in my chair again. "Let's just talk about my ideas and then go from there, okay?"

Jeffrey visibly relaxes and then clasps his hands in front of him on the table. "Okay. Sounds good."

"Now, I think there are a few things I need to see in order to offer constructive feedback," I begin, knowing that I put some deep thought into this over the past twenty-four hours. Once I knew I was going to go through with this, I kept thinking about my own dates, ones that had revealed aspects of my prospective partners that instantly turned me off. I also want to observe Jeffrey in different settings to see if he knows how to control his charismatic personality, which can be an asset to him if he knows when and where to let it out. The one thing I'm not sure how to measure is how he is with women *physically*, but I figure we can cross that bridge when we get to it.

You want to cross that bridge now, Ariel, don't you?

Shut up, conscience. Whose side are you on, anyway?

"Like . . . ?" he asks.

"I think we should go on a few pseudo-dates so I can feel you out, and then from there, I'm sure I'll be able to pinpoint what we can focus on to help you get the girl of your dreams."

Jeffrey rubs his hands together. "I can get on board with that. And what exactly will you be looking for?"

I shake a finger at him. "Nope. I'm not going to tell you because then you'll change how you act. Let's just take it one date at a time, and then, if I see something alarming, I'll correct you in the moment."

"Sounds easy enough."

"If this is so easy, then why do you need my help?" I challenge him, which takes him by surprise.

"Well, uh . . . that's not what I meant. I just . . ." Watching him squirm may become my new favorite pastime.

"Relax, Jeffrey. I'm just teasing you."

He sighs. "Ariel, I don't think I've ever met a woman who can keep me on my toes like you can."

I giggle. "I hope that's a good thing."

He leans forward in his seat now, grinning from ear to ear. "I'm almost positive that it is."

I remind my heart not to gallop like a horse blazing through a field as I finish my tea and Jeffrey and I make small talk. Once I get up to toss my cup in the trash, Jeffrey follows me outside. It's a clear summer night in San Diego, the cool breeze offering a reprieve from the heat of the day. Even in the thick of summer, San Diego offers the most beautiful weather around, one of the many perks of living here.

I stare at anything but Jeffrey, which has him breaking our silence quickly. "What are you looking at?"

Walking side by side, I stare ahead as I speak. "People. I could people-watch all day."

"Really?"

"Oh, yeah. I love wondering what their stories are, especially couples." I discretely point to the side, where a man who is blatantly much older than the woman he's with follows her around holding numerous shopping bags. "For instance, I'd say she's at least fifteen years younger than him and she's the much younger secretary that he left his wife for."

"You think so?"

"Maybe. Or that's her dad . . ."

"The math doesn't add up on that one, Ariel," Jeffrey says, "but I'm betting you're right about them on some level."

"I could be wrong, too," I say, shrugging and then finding another couple, probably in their seventies, sitting next to each other on a bench, eating ice cream in silence. "What about them?" I point so Jeffrey knows where I'm looking.

"High school sweethearts, married for over fifty years. They're so comfortable with each other that they don't even have to talk anymore."

"That, or he doesn't have his hearing aid turned on so he can't hear her," I joke, which makes him laugh.

"That is possible, too." We slide into silence again before he changes the subject. "So, what are you up to for the rest of your night?" Jeffrey asks as we continue to stroll down the sidewalk of the shopping center. As we turn a corner, a courtyard full of plants, benches, and pergolas for smaller vendors reveals itself, filled with even more people I could watch and create stories about all evening. But my pajamas and a tub of Ben and Jerry's are calling my name.

"Netflix and chill for me."

His eyebrows lift. "Oh, you're speaking my language now. Care for some company?"

I scoff. "Sorry, I Netflix and chill just fine on my own." He doesn't respond with a quirky comeback, so I flip the interrogation on him. "What about you?"

"I have quite the drive back to LA, unfortunately."

That stops me in my tracks. "You don't live in San Diego?"

"Nope. I've been living in a LA for a while now, mostly because of my job. But I don't mind coming down here, especially to see Joselyn . . . and now you."

"So you're going to drive down here every time we meet up?" The thought that this would be an inconvenience to him didn't occur to me.

He nods confidently. "Yup."

"That's like a two-hour drive with no traffic."

"I know," he says, casting his eyes over to me before smirking. "But it's worth it."

My heart doesn't know how to take his admission, but luckily the fountain up ahead offers me a distraction. We were both headed to the parking lot anyway, but now that I've seen the fountain, I can't leave until I follow through with my routine.

"Do you mind if we stop here really quick?" I ask, reaching into my purse to find my wallet.

"Sure. You need to make a wish or something?" he teases.

"Um, yeah, I do, actually." Watching for his reaction, I flip my eyes to his for a moment before opening the coin purse on my wallet and fishing around for a few pennies. Normally, I save pennies for this sort of thing, but I'm not opposed to using a nickel, dime, or even a quarter in a pinch.

"Wait. You're serious."

"As a heart attack." I locate a penny for each of us and hand one to him, noticing his face twisted up in confusion. "Come on. Make a wish with me, and then I'll explain later."

Shrugging, he follows me to the edge of the fountain where I close my eyes, telepathically share my wishes with the universe, and then toss the coin into the water, only opening my eyes when I hear the plop of the metal breaking through the surface.

I turn to Jeffrey, who was apparently watching me the entire time. "Your turn."

"I can't decide what to wish for. I feel like there's all this pressure on me in the moment."

Chuckling, I ask, "Did I catch you that off guard?"

"Well, yeah. And now I'm at war. Do I wish for something totally unrealistic like a flying pony? Or something more likely to come true, like a kiss from the girl I'm currently standing next to?"

I narrow my eyes at him. "I think you'll have better luck with the pony."

He shrugs his shoulders. "Well, can't blame a guy for trying."

Closing his eyes, he mumbles something under his breath and then flicks the coin into the water, which lands just to the right of where mine did. "You're not going to ask me what I wished for, are you?"

"Nope. You can't share your wish aloud, otherwise it won't come true." I twist on my heels and start heading in the direction of my car again as Jeffrey finds his place at my side once more.

"Okay, so spill. What's with the wishing in fountains?"

Sighing, I shove my hands in the pockets of my jean shorts. "It's something I've been doing since I was a little kid. My mom turned me on to it, saying that you should never pass by a fountain without making a wish. And I don't know . . . it just stuck with me." I glance a sneak peek at him, meeting his eyes that haven't left my face since I started talking. "Now, I make it a point to always have change on me and take a moment to put out some hope in the world, whether it's for me or someone else."

"So the ice queen does have a soft side . . ." he jokes.

I poke my finger at his chest. "Yeah, but don't go around sharing that with everyone, all right? The only reason you know is because I couldn't leave without tossing a coin in. It's almost like a superstition of mine."

I don't elaborate on how my mother used wishes as a way to instill hope back in me after my dad left. I don't explain that most of my wishes were for him to return until I finally realized he wasn't coming back. And I don't whisper that today I wished for Jeffrey to prove me wrong—that throughout this little arrangement between us, I hope he can prove to me that not all men are slime. Whether or not that results in the two of us ending up together is still up for debate, but at least Jeffrey could potentially put some faith back in *my* world concerning men and love, even though I'm not sold on the idea entirely anyway.

"I pick up every coin I find on the sidewalk," he says, pulling me from my thoughts.

"Really?"

"Yup," he nods, looking forward now as we walk. "I used to only pick up the ones that showed heads because apparently those are the lucky ones. But now, I pick them all up but put them in two separate jars—one for heads up and the other for tails. The tails ones I donate to a local charity when the jar gets full, but the heads I keep like trophies, like all that luck has to make something happen in my life at some point." And then, as if he manifested it, he stops dead in his tracks, bends over, and plucks a coin off the ground, one displaying heads. Grinning from ear to ear, he turns to me, showing me the penny. "See? You must be my lucky charm, Ariel, because I haven't found one heads up in a long time."

I playfully shove him. "That was cheesy."

"You liked it," he says as he leans closer.

And he's right. I do. I like his cheesiness, but I can't let him know that. Not right now.

"So, what do you think would happen if I tossed this coin in the fountain? Do you think that would guarantee my wish to come true?"

I glance back at the fountain several yards behind us now. "I don't know. None of my wishes have ever come true, so I don't think it matters . . ."

His face falls. "Really?"

I lift my shoulders up and down quickly. "Yeah, but wishing is just a silly, childish thing to do, anyway. Like I said, I do it more now out of habit than anything."

Slowly, he reaches out and lifts my chin with two of his fingers. "Maybe your luck has been saving up too then, just like my coins. One of these days, your wish is bound to come true, Ariel. I firmly believe that."

Suddenly, it feels hard to breathe. My legs become shaky, my mouth grows dry, and swallowing becomes a chore.

Intense want radiates from my chest for this man that I barely know but feel like knows *me*—sees me. He listens and pays attention. His humor and easygoing nature are something so foreign that I feel like he's making me remember that not everyone lives their life like I do with a shield up at all times.

He's honest. Funny. And attractive.

There, I said it.

His smile, his fierce green eyes, and the thick head of dirty blond hair that he can't help but run his hand through from time to time.

I'm attracted to him—and that's what's scaring me more than anything.

I watch his eyes drift to the side, and then he releases my chin. Walking over to one of the planters lining the sidewalk, he plucks a bloom of hydrangeas and brings them back over to me.

Reaching for me, he tucks the few flowers behind my ear, and my pulse picks up speed as I feel his fingers move my hair out of the way and his skin makes contact with mine. I swear I forget how to breathe as he gently places the stem securely.

His lips are millimeters from my own, his scent so strong that it's almost like I'm immersed in a bubble of just him and me in this moment. All the people around us fade away as I focus on his movements, the stubble on his jaw, and the way his tongue darts out slowly to lick his lips.

"Thank you for agreeing to help me, Ariel."

His words finally bring me back to reality, out of the daydream I was just having about kissing him.

Uh, there will be no more of that, Ariel. Reel it in, girl.

"You're welcome. Don't make me regret this," I bite back, trying to bring some levity to the moment while fighting like hell to raise my protective shield again.

"Oh, I don't plan on it."

Suddenly, I'm the one with regrets.

Too much about him draws me in, but it's too late to back out now. I told him I'd help him. I committed to spending time with him, so that's what I'm going to do. I just hope that my resolve doesn't completely crumble in a way I can't recover from. I've been broken twice. The third time definitely won't be a charm.

~

"Mom?" I call out once I walk through the front door of our house. Yes, I still live with my mother, but she's also my best friend. It's been her and me against the world since I was ten years old. Once Dad showed his true colors and left us, we clung to each other to survive. Looking back on it now, I can see how sharing a home with my mother might be playing into my lack of a dating life. But even when I was with my ex, I was able to navigate the circumstances and have a relationship—until he showed his true colors, too.

"In the kitchen," she replies as I hang up my purse on the hook by the door, take my shoes off and place them on the rack on the floor, and then head in her direction. When she sees me, her eyes instantly light up. "You're home late today."

"I had a meeting after work that I had to go to."

She eyes me warily. "Was this meeting a date?"

Rolling my eyes, I move toward the cupboard to grab a glass for water. As I fill it from the dispenser on the front of the fridge, I say, "No. Not a date." Not yet, anyway, although all I thought about was Jeffrey on my drive home.

"Shame. You should be out dating on a Friday night, Ariel. Not hanging at home with your mother."

I turn to face her. "One, I happen to like hanging with my mom." She smiles but rolls her eyes right back at me. "And two, dating is a waste of time and something I no longer see as a realistic investment."

"Honey..."

"No, Mom. We've been through this. Guys suck."

"Not all men suck, Ariel."

"I don't see you getting out there and dating after what Dad did to you. To us."

"That's because I was raising you. It's not that I didn't have options, but I'll be the first to admit that I was scared to put myself out there again for a very long time. But now, I'm trying. I've actually been talking to someone online for a while now."

I nearly drop the glass of water in my hand. "What?" This is news to me, blindsiding me after years of thinking Mom and I were on the same wavelength about love.

"His name is Vincent. He's a single parent like I am, although his wife died five years ago, so our circumstances are slightly different. But I like him, and we're planning on meeting each other soon."

"Holy shit, Mom."

She closes the distance between us, placing her hands on my shoulders. "I know that your father hurt you, and that ex-boyfriend of yours wasn't any better. But you can't make all men pay for what they did. Besides, you are a beautiful, vibrant, genuine, and intelligent young woman. There will be a man someday who will appreciate all of that about you."

Jeffrey's face pops into my mind as her words stop, but I quickly push it away. "I like being alone."

She huffs. "You're not alone, Ariel. You have me. And that will never change. But I'd hate to see you not live your life or take chances on love because you've been burned. It's our willingness to keep putting ourselves out there that matters, sweetheart. You can't find love if you don't give it a chance to find you, too."

I bite on my bottom lip. "You're really going to try dating again?"

"I already have been. At least online, that is. But yes, darling. I'm only in my fifties. I still have plenty of life to live, and I'd love to find someone else to share it with."

"I'm not good enough for you, then," I tease her.

"Of course, honey. But you're going to have your own life someday, and I want my own, too. That doesn't change the fact that you and I will always be close. It's been you and me against the world for almost twenty years, Ariel. And I wouldn't have changed it for anything."

"You wouldn't change what Dad did?"

She contemplates her answer for a moment. "Honestly, no, and here's why. What your father did—hiding another family from us, pretending to be someone he wasn't, lying about who he is—that was more about his own issues than the two of us doing anything wrong. It took me a long time to understand that, but it's the truth. I've forgiven him for my peace of mind, but it wasn't something I did or you did that made him make that choice. And that's what matters. Just because he betrayed me doesn't mean every man will."

"Wow. Why haven't you ever said anything about this before?"

"Because I was still coming to grips with it. And lately, I feel like you've become more reclusive and less willing to live your life. You need to get out of this house, Ariel. Time is passing. And as much as I love spending it with you, you need to find your own path, too. We can't live together forever."

"Why not?" I whine, which makes her laugh.

"Because one day soon, I want to get laid without my daughter overhearing."

"Oh my God!" I shout, setting my glass on the counter so I can plug my ears. "Mom!"

"What? I still have needs, my dear. And I know you do, too!"

"Dear God, please, stop talking before my ears bleed."

My mom cackles as she removes my fingers from my ears. "Promise me you'll do something out of your comfort zone soon, or I'll keep saying more things about my sex life."

"Okay, okay! I promise!"

"Good. Now, I'm off for my video chat with Vincent." Only then do I realize she's curled her hair, has a full face of makeup, and has one of her favorite blouses on. "I'll see you in the morning."

"Good night, Mom." I kiss her on the cheek and then make my way toward the couch, debating which show I'm going to continue watching until I pass out while wondering what the hell just happened and how ironic it is that she had that conversation with me on the same night I agreed to this ruse with Jeffrey.

When my dad left, I watched my mother change. I saw how secluded she became, how she would hide in the bathroom to cry at night and how the light in her eyes seemed to vanish. And even though she thought she was keeping her emotional turmoil from me, I felt it. I felt how sad and hopeless she'd become. I watched her shut off parts of herself.

She got better as time went on, but even when I would make jaded comments about my father, she tried to keep optimism in her voice. Over time, her light came back, and part of me thinks she did it for me. But now, her light is shining again for herself. I guess since she never tried dating again, I assumed she was happy just being the two of us, alone together.

She's right, though. She's still a vibrant woman who has needs, so should I think the same thing about myself? Lord knows I've been reluctant to even think about men after my breakup two years ago. Is it finally time to get back in the saddle and try to date again?

Even if Jeffrey isn't the man for me, at least helping him will also help me. It will force me out of my comfort zone, grant me the courage to live my life instead of staying home every night, wondering if I'm destined to be alone forever. And it will allow me to find that girl deep inside who still believes in love—the one who watched Disney movies as a kid and cried every time the couple got their happily ever after. Now, I just read about it in books, and the fairy tales are a little dirtier.

Halfway through an episode of *Good Girls*, I hear my mother laughing through her door, a genuine laugh that I can't remember hearing for the longest time. Sure, we laugh together and have fun. But this laugh—it is one full of hope, of falling for someone. And that's when I realize she's right. It's time to take a risk.

Little does she know, I'm risking a lot with the agreement I made with Jeffrey. But perhaps I do need to risk my heart a bit, too. And maybe he can be the man to show me that the risk is worth the reward.

Chapter 5

Jeffrey

"You ready to go to lunch?" Damien pops his head into my office as I keep tapping away on my computer.

"Yeah, just give me a minute. Let me finish this email."

"I got the contract finalized for the Pampers account, by the way," he says, stepping through the door and into the room. "I can't believe we're signing them as a client."

"I can't believe that we're going to be selling diapers," I chide. "From period products to diapers. Never thought I'd see the day."

Damien chuckles as I hit send and stand up from my chair. "Dude, you and me both. But that's what happens when you fall in love with a woman and have children. The world and your priorities become entirely different."

"Speak for yourself," I mutter, tamping down the jealousy I feel whenever I think about how ridiculously happy my best friend is.

Damien and I became fast friends the first day I started working at Goldstein Advertising eight years ago. We were both fresh out of college, eager to make names for ourselves, hungry for accolades and money. Working on the same team, we realized that we bounced ideas well off each other and shared a lot of the same interests. Hell, if Damien were a woman, he'd be fucking perfect for me. But alas, neither of us swing that way, so instead, we developed a bromance that has helped us both professionally and personally.

Three years ago, I witnessed Damien fall head over heels for his childhood nemesis, Charlotte. The two of them grew up together in South Carolina, but both moved to California for college. When they crossed paths, Damien and I were trying to win the Remedy account, a company that makes menstrual products. Damien lied to our boss that he had a girlfriend since Dave wasn't sure we could appeal to the company due to our lack of female companionship, and the rest was history. Their fake-dating ruse turned into an unconditional love any man could hope to find one day—a man like me.

"Hey." Damien moves closer, resting his hand on my shoulder. "You'll find your person, Jeffrey."

"Can't hear that enough." I reach for my wallet and keys as Damien stares at me.

"You will. I have faith in that, man."

"Thanks. But it's easy to be optimistic when you have a wife and kid, Damien. You're ridiculously happy and content with your life. Try being single nowadays. It's exhausting and extremely debilitating."

"What happened with Ariel, then? Did she turn your proposition down?"

We walk down the halls of our office toward the elevator, stepping in once the doors open. "Actually, she agreed."

He eyes me suspiciously. "Then why aren't you dancing around your office to eighties pop? Or belting out love ballads? You practically shattered glass with your scream the other day when she called you to meet up, remember?"

Laughing off his recollection of my reaction, I say, "Yeah, I know. But now . . ." I shake my head. "I'm not sure I should go through with it."

With intense thought etched on his features, Damien turns to me. "Let's get some food in our stomachs and then talk this out."

Once we arrive at one of our favorite lunch spots, The Chop Shop, we place our orders, take a seat at our usual table, and wait for our food to arrive while sipping on our peach mango iced tea.

"Okay, talk to me. What's the holdup? Last time you spoke of this girl, you were optimistic and determined."

"Dude. I fucking like her, okay?"

Damien narrows his eyes at me, his brow furrowed. "Yes, I thought that was established."

"Like, I *really* fucking like her." Spinning my cup around, I stare at it instead of meeting Damien's gaze. "And you know what happens every time I let myself get excited about a woman, man. It ends the same way—me being friend-zoned or ghosted, wondering what the hell I did wrong."

Damien tips his chin in understanding. "I see."

"And even though it seemed like a good idea at the time—convincing her to coach me on dating so we could spend time together—now, I'm second-guessing it. The other night, when we met up, she opened up about something important to her, and it struck a chord with me. She's an actual person; I don't want to deceive her."

Walking through the shopping center with Ariel Friday night was so easy, natural, and fun, and then, when she made a wish in that fountain, something shifted in my chest. An innocence about her was revealed, even though she tried to pass it off as no big deal. But it changed things for me. I didn't just want to kiss the woman senseless, I wanted to know everything about her—her wants and desires, what she wants her future to look like, and just like the first time I met her, I wanted to make her laugh more than anything, to bring back that smile on her face that feels like a beacon of light calling me home.

I just fucking want her.

"I get it. I felt that way with Charlotte. Like, it was supposed to be fake, but it turned real for me very quickly."

"It's been real for me from the beginning. I can't explain it because my reaction to her has been different from the moment I met her. She's so guarded, but all I want to do is knock down those walls I know she's built so damn high to keep people out. She has a quirky sense of humor that only shines through at certain moments, but I fucking live for it. Because otherwise, she's reluctant to let her true self show. And she's goddamn gorgeous, man. One of those women who doesn't even have to try because her natural beauty is so eye-catching, you can't help but stare."

"Damn, you have it bad, my friend."

I huff out a laugh. "I know. And that's why I'm not sure if this is a good idea—because if I'm already second-guessing this, that means I'm going to end up disappointed like every other time."

"You don't know that. I mean, if the woman is letting her guard down around you, that's a good sign to begin with, man. And you even said so yourself—the reason you convinced her to 'help' you was so you could spend time with her without creating the pressure of dating."

"I know, but you don't think I'm misleading her?"

He weighs his head from side to side. "Yes and no. I think you should just go with it, feel her out, and if you sense her feelings are changing toward you, be honest with her. Tell her that you're not interested in anyone else, just her. You can tell her that your feelings shifted, even though they've been there from the beginning, but you didn't want to scare her."

"Sounds simple enough." His words, although straightforward, alleviate a little bit of the stress I've been under all weekend. After my meeting with Ariel on Friday, I've been questioning my plan. This is what happens when you react in the moment and say things without thinking, a circumstance I've found myself in numerous times in my life. And you'd think I would have learned my lesson by now, but sadly, here I am again.

"I just want this to work. I want her. I've never felt this pressure with a woman before, but that just tells me the stakes are high."

"Then just be yourself."

"Ha. Look how well that's worked out for me in the past."

Damien snaps his fingers in front of my face to garner my attention. "Jeffrey, you don't want a woman who can't accept you for you. Bottom line. So if she wants you to be yourself, then do it. Don't hold back. Be the quirky, no-filter guy that I've grown to love."

That has me smiling and borderline crying in our favorite lunch establishment. "Aw, I love you, too, man."

Damien chuckles. "I know you do. Now, tell me what you have planned for your first date. You said you're meeting up this week, right?"

"Yeah, Friday night. I didn't want to try to squeeze a date in during the middle of the week, especially with the commute."

"Agreed. So where are you gonna take her?"

"Well, she mentioned she loves to people-watch." My lips lift in a smile as I recall her creating stories about the people around us last Friday night. "So I was thinking a karaoke bar. There's no better source of entertainment, in my opinion."

"I like it. It's fun, low pressure. You can have a couple of drinks, laugh, get to know each other a bit more. I think it's a good idea."

"Yeah?"

"Confidence is key, my man. Show her that you have faith in

yourself, that you have something to offer her, and the rest will fall into place."

Nodding, I take a long drag of my iced tea just as our food arrives. "Okay, Damien. I'm gonna give it my all. Here's hoping that's enough this time."

~

"I hope you can handle people singing off-key," I say to Ariel as I hold open the door to the bar, waiting for her to walk through.

It's eight o'clock, so the crowd isn't too big yet, but this place had great reviews online for their karaoke night, so I'm sure the atmosphere will improve as time goes on.

"Can *you* handle it, Jeffrey?"

"There's a lot I can handle, Ariel," I say, hoping she can sense the double meaning of my words. After my lunch with Damien, I made sure to dig deep and find that confidence I felt was lacking. And lucky for me, as soon as I picked up Ariel from her house tonight, it rushed back to me.

My tongue nearly fell out of my mouth when I saw her. Dressed in tight denim jeans and a black top that shows the perfect amount of cleavage, her hair down in soft waves around her face that just crest the tops of her shoulders, and gold hoop earrings hanging from her ears, Ariel is fucking perfection. Simple yet sexy. Gorgeous yet understated.

She doesn't try too hard, and that's one of the things that drew me to her in the first place. She doesn't put on an act. She isn't afraid to speak her mind. And she sure as hell doesn't realize how enticing she is to a man like me. I'm looking for something real, and she's about as real and honest as it gets.

"Perfect. So let's see how you can handle your alcohol then, shall we?" she asks as I follow her deeper into the bar, watching her scope out a booth before we both slide into our respective sides.

"Is this part of my test?"

"Yes and no. I honestly just want to see if you can keep a straight face while you take a shot."

I knock on the wooden table between us. "I'll have you know I was a straight A student in school, and I barely even studied." I wince. "But in college, I may have been known as the man who lost his clothes once tequila was involved."

Ariel snorts, a quirk of hers I find endearing. "Well, then, I guess I know what we're ordering."

"Don't say I didn't warn you," I toss back at her. "When you get a glimpse of all this," I continue, waving my arm down my torso, "just make sure you can control yourself."

Her eyes bounce up and down my body as she bites her lip, a move that has me wondering if she's as attracted to me as I am to her. I remember the way she averted her gaze that day in my sister's dressing room when I changed my shirt. But this look—it's much more intentional, flirtatious even. Could it be that Ariel is trying this date on for size just like I am?

Maybe Damien was right. I go through with this the way I intended and hope to God she sees that I'm the real deal.

"I think I'll be okay." Her smirk has me grinning myself as I watch her eyes glance around the rest of the bar.

A waitress comes by, and Ariel orders four shots of tequila and two waters for us.

"Are you hungry, too?"

"I can always go for food," she replies.

"We'll take an order of buffalo wings and nachos, too, then, please."

The waitress nods. "You got it."

"Good choices," Ariel says, pulling my attention back to her just as the waitress drops off our waters.

"Two of my favorites."

"You didn't ask if that was okay with me, though . . ."

Running my hand through my hair, I realize I've already fucked up. "Shit. I'm sorry."

"It's okay. Some girls don't like that, though. You may just want to check in with your date next time."

Hopefully, I won't have to do this with anyone else when our little agreement is over, but I still make a mental list for next time.

"Noted. I can change the order still if you want," I say, moving to stand from my side of the booth and chase the waitress down.

Ariel rests her hand on mine that's flat on the table, stopping me. "It's fine. I'm good with it. Just . . . trying to offer advice like you wanted, right?"

Slowly, I sit back down in my seat. "Yeah. Right." Clearing

my throat, I reach for my water, taking a large drink. "So, before the festivities begin, I think we should get to know each other more."

"You don't have to act so formal, Jeffrey. Relax. A girl doesn't want her date to feel like an interview."

Sighing, I lean back. "Fuck, I keep messing this up, don't I?"

"No." She bites her lip. "Maybe I just need to let you talk instead of interrupting and correcting you." She taps the table with her fingers. "I guess I'm just a little nervous, too."

"Why are you nervous?" I genuinely want to know, because in my mind, she doesn't have anything to lose here. She's not the one who's trying to change my mind about how she feels.

Contemplating her answer, her eyes finally meet mine. "It's been a long time since I've been out on a Friday night like this," she explains. "With a man, you know."

"Really?"

"Yes. And even though I know this isn't a real date, it still has me antsy. I mean, my boobs are on display," she says, gesturing to her cleavage that I've been fighting not to stare at since I picked her up. "I don't typically dress like this. I put makeup on, for crying out loud, and I'm wearing shoes that aren't sneakers. I feel completely out of my element."

"Ariel," I say sternly, making sure her eyes are locked on mine before I continue. "You look fucking phenomenal. Your boobs are perfect." She laughs. "And you have no reason to be nervous. It's just me, Jeffrey, your . . . friend, remember?" *Dude, did you just friend-zone yourself?*

"Right . . ." Her voice trails off as if she doesn't believe that statement, but I don't want her to debate it too much.

Luckily, our food comes right then, ending our confession session and giving us something to focus on other than nerves. "So how did you end up working for Greenlight Studios?"

Ariel finishes chewing her bite of buffalo wing before answering. "I've always been fascinated by television and movie production. My mom won tickets to *The Ellen Show* when I was fifteen, and being in the audience and seeing the whole production process was eye-opening for me. I realized then and there that I wanted to do that, be the person behind the scenes who makes everything run. I started off small as an intern, then a runner, and now, your sister's assistant, but I am trying to work my way up to be a producer someday. There's a ladder you kind of have to climb, but I'm not giving up now."

Damn. Driven, hardworking, and talented. Add those to the list of why I want to date this woman right now, please.

"And do you like working for my sister?" I ask, realizing that I don't know how she even became Joselyn's assistant.

"I love it, actually. When I got hired at the studio, I didn't do so with the intention of being an assistant to a talk show host, but when the position opened up, I applied. Your sister is someone I look up to immensely, actually, which helped make the decision for me."

"I look up to her, too," I reply as her eyes widen. "How could you not? Joselyn is one of those rare, genuine people in the world. Granted, she is my twin, so we must have that in common, right?"

Ariel smiles, a smile so natural it makes me beam with pride. My words made her do that. "Smooth. But she is. And she's even more genuine when her cohost is pissing her off."

That comment has me tossing my head back in laughter. "Oh, Hunter. Hayden says he's just putting on a front, but is he really that bad?"

"He ate the last blueberry muffin in front of her the other day."

I shudder. "Oh, fuck. That couldn't have gone over well."

She giggles, and the sound goes straight to my dick. "Yeah. But you're right. Being around your sister has helped me realize the type of woman I want to be: bold, opinionated, confident—"

"You are that woman, Ariel."

She scoffs. "I definitely don't feel like it. Lately, I just feel . . . jaded," she says on an exhale before her eyes widen as she realizes what she just revealed.

"Well, that's where I come in, right?" I say, dropping a nacho in my mouth as she does the same. I finish chewing and then declare, "That was my responsibility in this agreement, remember? To help you let loose."

Just then, the waitress brings our shots. "Sorry, the bar was backed up. Everything else okay?"

"Do you need anything?" I ask Ariel, and she smiles at my question.

"A few extra sides of ranch would be nice, please."

The waitress promises to return as Ariel slides two of the shots over to me. "You learn quickly, Jeffrey. Good move asking me if I needed anything before answering for us both."

I tap my temple with my finger. "Told you. Straight A student over here."

She lifts one of the shots toward me for a toast. I grab one of my own and meet her halfway. "What shall we toast to?" she asks.

"How about having fun and getting what we both want?"

She nods, her lips spreading in a grin again. "I like it."

"And your boobs," I add, dropping my eyes to her cleavage to absorb them fully now.

"My boobs?"

"Yup. I know you said you weren't sure about them, but I am. I'm definitely sure that they look fucking amazing, and I might not be able to stop staring at them all night, Ariel. Friends or not."

Her cheeks turn red right before my eyes. *Fuck, yes.* Seems I do have an effect on her. That's a good fucking sign.

"Well, I guess I can get on board with that toast, then."

We clink our glasses together, and I then take down the alcohol, feeling the burn course all the way down my throat. "Dear God. I can't remember the last time I took a shot!"

Ariel cackles across the booth. "Same. It seemed like a good idea at the time, but now I'm questioning my sanity." She grabs the other two shots, sliding one to me. "Quick. Let's just do the second one now and get it over with."

"For your sake, I hope this doesn't make the food we just ate make a reappearance."

"I agree."

We clink our glasses again and toss back the second shot,

which surprisingly goes down easier than the first one, covering my skin in a warmth as the alcohol hits me. "Fuck."

"Woo!" Ariel exclaims, slapping the table. "I hope I don't regret that tomorrow."

We both eat a little bit more food, making small talk in between bites, and that's when my eyes land on the pool tables in the corner of the bar. "Wanna play some pool before karaoke starts?"

She spins to find the pool tables I just set my sights on. "That depends; can you handle losing to a girl?"

I fake being shocked, dropping my jaw open and placing my palm on my chest. "Wow. That's awfully cocky of you, gorgeous. Are you saying you possess skills in the beautiful game of billiards? Does that mean you're about to kick my ass? I'll have you know, I am a bit skilled at the game myself."

Ariel tosses her head back as she laughs, clearly loosening up with me. And that's exactly what I wanted to happen. "Prepare to take a bruise to your ego, Jeffrey. You're about to know what it feels like to eat your words."

Chapter 6

Ariel

"Shit." I fall to the ground, my ass slamming down on the hardwood, clutching my foot in my hand as my toes throb to the same pace as the beat of my heart.

"Oh my God, Ariel. Are you okay?" Jeffrey slides down on his knees in front of me, looking panicked.

That cool confidence of his from before just came screeching to a halt as he took his shot during our game of pool, underestimated the force behind his cue, and sent the nine ball careening off the pool table, landing square on my big toe that I'm pretty sure is now broken.

"Um, not exactly," I wince, hissing through my words. Unwrapping my fingers from my foot, I stare down at the purple flesh that's swollen beyond its normal size.

"Fuck." Jeffrey reaches up and tugs on his hair, clearly full of remorse. "I'm so fucking sorry, Ariel. It was an accident." He bites on his bottom lip so hard I think he might draw blood.

"I know, Jeffrey. I know. I just didn't anticipate you launching a pool ball at my big toe tonight." Honestly, if this is what happens on his dates, I can see why he strikes out. Unfortunately, there are women who would cut ties with him after this. But I know Jeffrey didn't mean any harm. It was an accident, and he clearly looks torn up about it.

"Here. Let's take off your shoe." He reaches for the clasp on the ankle of my wedges that I wore since I was trying to dress up for tonight, a detail that I didn't need to follow through with but am glad I did, especially after taking in Jeffrey's reaction to my attire. And the man even made a toast to my boobs, so I'm guessing I did a good job on my outfit choice.

"No, Jeffrey . . . don't . . ." I try to get out before dissolving into a fit of giggles.

"Just let me look at it." He says as his fingers stroke the arch of my foot, launching me into a panic attack because I am ticklish, ticklish beyond measure. "Can we get some ice over here?" he calls over his shoulder to one of the waitresses as I struggle to breathe.

"Jeffrey," I say between laughs, "let go of my foot." But before he can comprehend what I'm saying, his finger moves again along my arch, sending my foot careening forward as I kick out in a panic again.

And unfortunately, my foot connects with his nose, throwing him backward as he lands on the floor with a thud.

"Oh my God!" I say, clasping my hands over my mouth when I realize what happened. "Jeffrey!"

I kicked him in the face. I bucked my heel against his nose.

Jesus, what is wrong with us?

I swear, if anyone else is watching this, I can only imagine what they see. A girl on her ass on the dirty floor of a bar with one shoe on and a giant purple toe and a man rolled onto his side, clutching his face as if he's just been kicked in the balls and face simultaneously.

I'm sure we make quite a hilarious sight.

Groaning, Jeffrey rolls to his side, removing his hands from his face long enough to see the blood pouring from his nostrils. "Shit."

"Crap." I struggle to stand then hobble on one shoe to a nearby table, stealing napkins from the people sitting there. "I'm sorry. We need these." Without waiting for their response, I shuffle back over to Jeffrey, kneeling down beside him, handing him the napkins as blood continues to pour from his nose onto the floor. "I'm so sorry, Jeffrey. I'm just so ticklish. I tried to warn you."

"Sure," he says from the floor, pushing himself up so I can see the teasing glint in his eyes. He shoves the napkins under his nose and then eyes me suspiciously. "You don't have to lie, Ariel. You can just tell me that you punted my face to get back at me for the pool ball landing on your toe. I can take it." He winks at me.

I playfully shove his shoulders before resting back on my ass, giving my knees a break from the hard surface below us. "Oh my God, Jeffrey. What the hell just happened?"

"Welcome to my luck in dating," he grates out, releasing the napkins from his nose to check to see if the bleeding has stopped. It hasn't, so he puts them back up to his nostrils.

"Well, I can't say that I've ever had something like this happen on one of my dates, bodily injuries and all."

He laughs and then moans after. "Shit. Don't make me laugh. You got me good, woman."

"I'm sorry."

"I'm sorry, too. Fuck, this wasn't how this was supposed to go."

A waitress comes by with ice for us at this moment, which we both graciously accept. "Let's go back to our table before the karaoke starts so we can get up off this floor," he says, and I nod in agreement.

Keeping the napkins under his nose, Jeffrey rises before me, reaching out with his free hand to help me up. And when I do, I land against his chest with a thud, gripping onto his shoulders for balance.

Being in his arms feels . . . *good*—too good. Despite the fact that one of my feet isn't even touching the ground right now and I can't see his mouth behind the napkins pressed against his face, my entire body goes warm, tingly even, just feeling his arm around my waist.

Jeffrey isn't the tallest man I've ever met, but he still has plenty of height on me considering I'm fairly short. All I can see right now are his blue eyes, darkened by the lack of lighting in the bar around us. But there's also lust in those deep blue pools of intrigue, lust I can feel radiating out of him as his hand tightens around my waist.

How could the man possibly want me after I almost just decapitated him?

"Are you okay to walk?" he asks, pulling me from my internal thoughts about what it would be like for him to claim me like this for real, to stake ownership over me in front of people and it actually mean something.

"Yeah, I think so." Holding my other shoe in my hand, we hobble over to our booth again.

The waitress comes by with more napkins for Jeffrey, which he quickly changes out. She takes his soiled ones away before bringing us two more shots of tequila. "On me. You two look like you could use it." With a wink, she saunters off.

"Guess we put on quite the show, didn't we?" Jeffrey teases, releasing the napkins from his nose now that the bleeding has stopped.

"At least we have flair."

Snorting, I reach for the shot. "Are you sure you're okay? Do you need to go to the bathroom or the hospital?"

Jeffrey shakes his head. "Nope. I'm fine. I'll live. It doesn't feel broken, so I think I'm good."

"Have you broken your nose before?"

"Yeah, in high school while playing baseball. I was pitching and got hit straight on in the face. I was lucky I didn't have to have surgery."

"Yikes," I say, even though the image of Jeffrey in a baseball uniform flashes through my mind. Why does that suddenly make him ten times hotter?

God, I bet he looks amazing in a baseball hat. And those pants.

Jesus, I'm way too hard up right now. It has to be the tequila—or perhaps my sanity left my body when the ball hit my foot.

"How's your toe?"

I glance down at my foot resting on the booth, still throbbing and swollen, and I place the bag of ice back on it. "I'll survive. There's not much you can do for a broken toe, anyway."

"Ladies and gentlemen! It's the moment you've been waiting for!" The emcee comes over the sound system, cutting off our conversation. "The event that we've been working toward for months has finally come together, and we're so honored to be hosting." Sensing a shift in the air, I take a good look around. And that's when I realize the clientele of this bar has drastically changed in the last hour, something Jeffrey and I were completely oblivious to while we were consumed in our pool game and its aftermath. My eyes bounce around the room as patrons start shrieking, dressed in attire that doesn't necessarily scream "let's go get some drinks at the neighborhood bar."

"Um, Jeffrey?"

"What?" he asks, wincing as he touches his nose.

"Did you happen to research what kind of karaoke was happening tonight?"

He drops his hand from his face, his eyes bugging out. "No. Why?"

"Welcome to the stage our first performer of the evening, a Miss Cherry Bing!"

Jeffrey and I both turn our heads in the direction of the stage where a very beautiful curvy drag queen steps up to the microphone dressed in a pink sequined dress, a black curly wig that would give Cher a run for her money, and a pink feathered boa.

He, I mean *she*, looks fabulous!

"Oh, shit," Jeffrey utters, twisting back to face me. "Um, this wasn't exactly what I had in mind so you could people-watch, Ariel."

Laughing, I start drumming my fingers on the table as Miss Cherry Bing belts out the first chorus of "It's Raining Men," a classic. "Who cares? This is better!"

Relief comes over Jeffrey's face, his eyes softening and his lips curving up into a smile. "Really?"

"Yes! Holy cow! This girl can sing!"

I can feel Jeffrey's eyes on me as I watch the performer on stage, but I'm too lost in the moment. I may have a broken toe, may have kicked my non-date friend in the nose and made him bleed, but this turn of events makes the entire night worth it.

"Glad you approve," he says, slicing through my attention. "It was all part of my master plan, anyway."

I smirk at him. "Your plan was to injure me and yourself and then hope that the drag queen karaoke was enough to turn the night around?"

Scratching his chin, I can hear his nails drag through the stubble along his jaw that gives him a slightly rugged look that I don't hate, especially right now in the dim lighting of the bar. "Well, did it work?"

I reach across the table and grab his hand, surprising us both. "Yeah, Jeffrey. It did."

Chapter 7

Jeffrey

"Dude. What the hell happened to your face?" Damien comes walking into my office first thing on Monday morning. It's back to the grind, but my face looks like it got put through a grinder, too.

Because I can't answer any question with an easy response, I reply, "I got in a bar fight, man. Some guy was hitting on Ariel, and I had to defend her honor, white knight style." Pretending to wield a sword, I swing my arm through the air.

Damien cackles. "Cut the shit. What really happened?"

Sighing, I stand from my desk and take off my suit jacket, draping it over the back of my chair. "Ariel kicked me in the face."

"What the hell? Why?" Damien asks through half-hearted laughter. "Please, tell me this was an accident."

"Oh, it was. But this was after I broke her toe—or at least almost did." Clutching his stomach, Damien laughs so loud that people all over our office floor are peering into my office. "Thanks for the support, man. Glad you can laugh at my expense."

Wiping tears from under his eyes, he says, "I'm sorry, but Jesus, Jeffrey. This would only happen to you, huh?"

I give him a sarcastic two thumbs-up. "Yup."

"So how did the night end?"

I smile, thinking about how much fun we ended up having despite those few obstacles. "Actually, pretty well. The karaoke bar ended up having an amateur drag queen night, and Ariel fucking loved it. We sat back in our booth, sang along to the songs, and hobbled out of the bar laughing and grinning from ear to ear. Then I took her home, hugged her goodnight, and that was that."

Damien crosses his arms over his chest. "That was it?"

"Yeah. Why?"

"She didn't offer you feedback on the date?"

Scratching my temple, I say, "No, actually. She didn't. Huh." His knowing smile has me questioning him. "What's that look for?"

"Well, I thought coaching you was the whole point of this? Why didn't she debrief the date with you at the end if that was the point?"

"I . . . I didn't even think about it. We were just having such a great fucking time, it must have slipped our minds."

He points a finger at me. "And that's a good sign, my friend."

"You think?"

"Yes. If she was so wrapped up in the evening that she forgot her part in all of this, I'd say you are making more headway with her than you think."

Hope surges in my chest as my smile follows its lead. "Damn, Damien. You just made my fucking morning."

He shrugs like it's no big deal. "Glad to be of service. And this means that you keep doing what you're doing, man. If she can roll with a broken toe, kicking you in the face, and drag queen karaoke, then you are making an impact."

"Fuck. I sure hope so."

"Hey, Melissa."

"Hey, Jeffrey. Two visits so close together? What a lucky sister!"

"Would you mind telling her that for me? It might help make up for all the times I shaved the hair off her Barbies' heads. Thanks."

Our conversation ends there on a laugh as I stride through the halls of stage twenty-four of Greenlight Studios, headed toward Joselyn's dressing room.

It's Friday, but I took a half day so I could head down and surprise Joselyn . . . and Ariel.

The woman has been on my mind all week, and I know that we made plans for tomorrow, but I was hoping that seeing her today would help the anticipation build.

I thought about texting her all week, asking her how her day was or if she ever started reading the book that I bought for her. But I chickened out. I was still on a high from last weekend and Damien's revelation about our "date," and I didn't want to ruin it. But this weekend, I plan on making more progress where she's concerned, starting with bringing my sister her favorite cupcakes from Grady's Bakery and the shortbread cookies from the coffee shop for both of them.

Whoever said the way to a man's heart was through his stomach must have clearly forgotten that women like to eat, too.

Knocking on Joselyn's door, I hear movement on the other side, whispering, and a loud bang before my sister opens the door, her hair wild around her face.

"Jeffrey?" Her eyes bulge out of her head as she looks over her shoulder and then back at me. "What . . . what are you doing here?"

"I came to visit and surprise you." Holding up the bag of bakery goods, I continue, "I brought cupcakes and cookies."

She purses her lips at me. "You know I can't turn down sugar." She opens the door wider and lets me in even though she appears hesitant to do so.

"Are you okay?" I drop my eyes down her body. "You look frazzled."

"Oh, yeah . . . I'm just . . . I was doing push-ups."

"Push-ups? In a dress?"

Her eyes move down her own body this time, taking in the turquoise dress she's wearing. "Um, yes. I just got a sudden urge, and then before I knew it, I was on my knees." Her eyes widen. "I mean, on the floor. No . . . uh . . ."

"And you say I'm the one who has trouble articulating themselves sometimes," I mutter, setting the bag of cupcakes and cookies on the coffee table in front of her couch.

My sister brushes her unruly hair from her face. "So, what are you doing here?"

"Well, I was supposed to come down to San Diego tomorrow to see Ariel, but I thought I'd make a weekend out of it and see you as well."

"You were coming to see Ariel?" she asks, placing her hands on her hips as she tilts her head.

"Yeah. She's, um, coaching me in dating," I say, trying to fight the grin on my face.

"Why do I feel like there's more to it than that?"

"Because there is." Sighing, I turn to face my sister head-on. "I asked her out, but she turned me down, Jos. She said we'd be better off as friends, which you know is like my fucking kryptonite. So, in a panic move I'm not entirely proud of, I convinced her to coach me on dating since I seem to keep striking out with women."

Her jaw falls open. "Jeffrey . . ."

Reaching up, I yank on my hair, which did look great a moment ago. But Joselyn's vocal disappointment has me feeling desperate all over again. "I know, but it was the only thing I could think of so I could at least spend time with her, maybe try to convince her that I can be more than her friend."

"You really like her, don't you?"

"I do, Jos." I drop my hands to my sides. "Tell me I'm not fucking pathetic and stupid."

She closes the distance between us, reaching for my left hand. "No, you're not pathetic and stupid. But I don't know if deceiving her is the right thing to do here. She clearly has trouble letting people in. What happens when she finds out you weren't entirely honest with her? How do you think that's going to go over?"

"I haven't thought that far ahead."

"Typical man." Shaking her head, she says, "Just be careful. I don't want to see you end up hurt again."

"Well, she already kicked me in the nose, so it's too late for that."

"What? How the hell did that happen?"

I launch into an explanation to bring my sister up to speed on the Ariel front when her dressing room door swings open and in walks our topic of discussion.

And fuck, she looks beautiful.

She's wearing denim jeans and a plain white tank top, and her shoulders are sun-kissed while her hair is pulled back in a ponytail. Her hazel eyes glitter under the lights and widen as soon as she sees me.

"Jeffrey? What . . . what are you doing here?"

"I came down a day early. I wanted to see Jos while I was here, but seeing you is an added bonus." Without thinking, I walk toward her and pull her in for a hug, pressing a soft kiss to her temple. I hear her breath hitch as she pulls back and looks up into my eyes.

"Oh. Hi," she says breathlessly, her eyes wide as saucers.

"Hi, yourself, sweetheart." Her mouth falls open as I bop her on the nose, turning toward my sister, who has a shit-eating grin on her face.

"So, you two are . . ."

"Friends," Ariel finishes for her, pushing herself off me and adjusting her shirt. "Just friends."

Joselyn narrows her eyes at her assistant and then at me. "I see. I had no idea that you two hit it off so well after that initial introduction—"

"I came to give you the schedule for next week," Ariel interrupts her. She takes a piece of paper off the clipboard she's holding and passes it to my sister. "Here is the list of guests and topics we have set in case you want to do some research over the weekend."

"Yes. Thank you. I will definitely take some time to prepare."

"Great," Ariel says a little too enthusiastically before shifting her eyes to me. "Well, I'll let you two catch up."

"Sounds good. And I'll see you tomorrow, Ariel, for my next coaching lesson. I think you're really helping me with this whole dating thing," I say, winking at her, which has her eyes bugging out of her head.

"Um. Yeah. See you then." Joselyn and I both watch her run off and slam the door shut behind her.

"I take it she didn't tell you about our arrangement, did she?" I ask, turning to face my sister again.

"Nope. I didn't even realize you two were hanging out at all until you told me just a few moments ago. But you'd best believe we'll be talking about it later."

"Don't be too hard on her. Remember, I'm trying to win her over."

Her face softens. "I know, Jeffrey. I'm just worried that you're trying to win over someone who doesn't want to be won."

∼

Shooting an icy glare across the table at me, Ariel takes a sip of her wine.

"Are you going to be mad at me all night?"

"I'm not mad."

"Could have fooled me," I say, taking a drink from my beer as well.

We're seated at a table covered by a white linen tablecloth in one of San Diego's most popular restaurants on the bay, Tom Ham's Lighthouse, commencing our Saturday night date. I surprisingly was able to get a reservation last week, and I knew this dinner date needed to be more romantic than our last one.

Floor-to-ceiling windows enclose the entire dining room, highlighting a breathtaking view of the bay. Boats bob in the water as the sun lights up the entire sky in hues of yellow and orange. The view is amazing, and my date looks even more gorgeous than the scenery around us.

But by the way the woman across from me is staring me down, our date is not exactly going the way I'd hoped.

When I picked up Ariel from her house, she barely made eye contact with me, but that didn't stop me from appreciating the way she looked. In a simple strapless black dress that shows off her shoulders and collarbone and hugs her petite curves I would love nothing more than to kiss and lick, she stole the breath from my lungs when she opened the door. Her hair is pulled into a low bun on her neck, and a few tendrils frame her face.

Simplicity is what makes this girl so fucking beautiful. She doesn't have to try hard at all to garner my attention, and the small pop of eye makeup she's wearing tonight is just making it harder to deal with the way she's staring at me. Her eyes look magnificent with the dusting of copper on her lids and mascara that's making her lashes even longer. And her lips—she's wearing a cherry gloss that makes me want to lick her mouth like a fucking ice cream cone.

I have to turn this evening around.

"Look, I'm sorry for whatever I did. I'm not sure what it was, but—"

"You told your sister about our arrangement," she cuts me off, folding her arms over her chest.

"Was I not supposed to? I mean, she's my sister, Ariel. We tell each other a lot. Not everything, but there's very little we hold inside. And I know she would be curious about why we were spending time together. If we're not actually dating, it's kind of hard to explain otherwise."

Her face softens a bit, but not enough for my liking. "I mean, I guess not. It's just that . . . you and I didn't discuss her knowing, and I would have appreciated you asking me first before you just blurted it out."

Ah. Now I see.

"I don't want this to create an issue with my job . . ."

Fuck, I didn't really think about it, even though I know she used that as an excuse not to date me in the first place. I was just so fucking excited to see her that my verbal diarrhea took over. And honestly, I tell my sister pretty much everything.

Reaching across the table for her hand, I wait until she puts hers in mine. And fuck, her skin is so soft, and she smells phenomenal—like berries and vanilla. Her scent is quickly becoming the oxygen I need to breathe.

Stroking my thumb over her fingers, I say, "I'm sorry. I didn't think it was that big of a deal. We're friends, right? Who cares what Joselyn thinks? You and I are doing this for our own reasons, so it shouldn't matter what other people say."

"Yes, but this is something you should definitely discuss with a woman you're seeing before taking it upon yourself to air their business, okay? Just for future reference, you know." She takes her hand back, leaving mine empty, identical to how my stomach just dropped like it was void of anything as well.

Clearing my throat, I sit back in my chair, feeling off-kilter again and a little annoyed that the progress I seemed to have been making with her feels like it was pulled out right from under me. And I really have no one to blame but myself. "Is that your advice as my coach?"

Her brow lifts. "Yes, it is."

"I see. So what about our last date? You never gave me any feedback after we said goodbye. That was almost a week ago.

Seems like a teacher wouldn't wait that long to offer their criticism if they wanted their student to really learn." I smirk at her across the table, sensing her discomfort rise as she wiggles in her seat, uncrossing her arms.

"Yes, well, I was busy."

"Me, too. But if this is going to work, I need to know what I'm doing wrong, Ariel. You had no problem telling me I was out of line airing our situation to my sister, so please, tell me what I need to be aware of so that the next woman I date isn't as pissed off at me as you are right now."

That makes her eyes turn to stone. The irritation in her gaze and stiffness of her body tells me she doesn't like that idea any more than I do. That means not all hope is lost. Hearing those words had an effect on her, just like they did to me.

Keep going, Jeffrey. Keep investing this time in her. She's bound to break at some point. She can only deny for so long that she's interested in you as more than just a friend.

"Well, let's start with the good stuff then." She reaches for her wine, taking a hefty drink and then setting her glass back down. "The bar was a good place of choice. Low pressure, a fun atmosphere. I wanted to see how you handled your alcohol, and you did well. You didn't get sloppy, took shots with me even though I know you didn't want to. And you played into my love of people-watching, which I appreciated."

"Glad to hear I passed the test."

"Honestly, what impressed me was how you handled both the beating we took and me beating you at pool." The corner of her mouth tips up. "Many other guys would have taken the hit to their ego a lot worse. You handled it . . . well."

Chuckling, I say, "I am no stranger to the shit that happens in my life, especially clumsiness and accidents. I guess I'm just used to it by now. But I'm glad to hear you think I'm progressing toward mastery of dating. By the way, how's your toe?"

She lifts her foot from under the table, highlighting the muscle tone in her calves as she flexes her foot, drawing my eyes to her black heels that I want to see wrapped around my back. "Healing nicely. I don't think it was broken, just bruised."

"Good to hear. I had two black eyes for a few days, by the way."

That has her smile finally making an appearance. "I'm sorry."

"Don't worry about it. I just told my coworkers I was in a fight defending your honor."

"I'm sure they believed you."

Leaning over the table, I say, "I would gladly take a beating for a woman who's mine. I can definitely put up a fight." I mock flexing my bicep. "I do work out, you know."

She licks her lips, fighting a smile. "That's very noble of you."

Resting back in my chair again, I redirect the conversation. "So, anything else?"

"Well, besides you ordering for me without asking, which you remedied very quickly . . . not really." She shrugs. "It wasn't a perfect date by any means, but it was . . . fun . . . which is most important."

Grinning, I stare at her. "So would you say I've been holding up my end of the bargain so far?"

"Yes. You have. And that's why I didn't have any feedback for you, Jeffrey. Because I honestly . . ." She exhales heavily. "I had a really great time."

"Those words are music to my ears." I grab my beer and hold it out to her, waiting for her to grab her wine, which she does. "Well, then. I say we move forward with our date this evening, and I give you more fun. And you stop being mad at me. Don't worry about my sister. She's not going to think any differently of you."

Taking a deep breath, she clinks her glass with mine. "Okay. I can do that."

We both take a drink of our beverages. "At least I know what your wrath feels like now."

She narrows her eyes at me. "Oh, Jeffrey. You have no idea how much worse it can get."

I visibly shiver. "Not sure I want to know then."

Her head tips back in laughter as the waiter comes by to take our order. We choose a lobster dip for an appetizer, Ariel orders a salmon fillet, and I order steak and scallops. This place is known for their exquisite seafood, and I can't wait to stuff my face—in an elegant way, of course.

Just after the appetizer shows up, she shifts the attention to me. "So how did you get into advertising?" she asks as she dips a piece of the crusty bread in our dip, blowing on it to cool before depositing it in her mouth. And my eyes are transfixed on her lips until I remember that I need to answer her question.

"Oh, that's easy. Super Bowl commercials."

She stops chewing. "What?"

"My dad has always been a huge football fan, so I grew up with a love of the sport as well. And as you know, the Super Bowl has some of the best commercials all year. I used to live for them. One day, I asked my father how someone gets their commercial to air during the Super Bowl, and he said they pay for advertising. And that's when I decided I wanted to work in advertising, and hopefully, one day, have a commercial air during the Super Bowl."

"Wow, I love that. Have you come close to that yet?"

"Well, my best friend and partner, Damien, and I have been working hard landing major accounts, but none have secured advertising during the Super Bowl yet. Although, we did just sign Pampers, so here's hoping that works out."

"The diaper company?"

"Yup."

"Wow, Jeffrey. That's huge. Congratulations."

"Thank you."

"Do you have any commercials out that I may have seen?"

"Actually, yes. Our first big one was with Remedy feminine products. The one of the young girl in the aisle of products at the store, with—"

"—her mom!" She cuts me off. "Oh my God, I loved that commercial. I thought it was so female positive. And the man standing there having no idea what to buy." She giggles. "It was perfect."

"That was actually inspired by Damien's real life."

She eyes me appreciatively. "I'm impressed. You certainly have a knack for the business then, don't you?"

I blow on my knuckles and then brush them on my shoulder. "I try."

"Oh my God. Don't do that again." Her laughter sounds as right as when you hit the jackpot on a slot machine.

"Too cheesy for you?"

"Yes. But then again, your cheesiness is growing on me."

Chapter 8

Ariel

"How do I keep losing?"

"You're too busy staring at my boobs, Jeffrey."

He stands to his full height again and shrugs. "Can't deny it, sweetheart. You've got a great rack."

"You're lucky I find your honesty refreshing."

"Well, if this were a real date, would you tell me not to look at the woman's boobs?"

Jealously rushes through me, but I tamp it down. "That depends on if you think the woman would welcome that kind of blatant ogling."

"Well, since we're friends, I feel like I can be honest with you. And the blush on your cheeks seems to indicate that you don't mind me looking all that much, do you?" He winks at me.

Even though his gaze is making me flustered, the thought of Jeffrey looking at another woman's chest is making me clench my jaw. But maybe it's a good reminder that this is temporary.

When he showed up yesterday at the studio to surprise Joselyn, she wasn't the only one caught off guard. The instant I saw him, my insides started flipping around like a little girl trying to nail a somersault on the playground. I'd been thinking about him all week and was eagerly awaiting our date tonight. But then he announced to his sister about our agreement, and I wanted to strangle him. Not because I'm embarrassed, but because I told Joselyn I wasn't interested in him, and agreeing to help him when I'm not interested seems a little odd—a detail I'm sure I'm going to have to explain to her come Monday.

Nevertheless, I couldn't stay mad at him for too long. It's the dimples. And the hair. God, when he runs his hands through it and it lays just perfectly each time, I want to simultaneously curse him for having impeccable locks and run my hands through it, ending with me pulling his lips toward mine for a kiss.

Yup. I'm officially lusting after the man I'm supposed to help date other women.

I know that Jeffrey meant no harm in being honest with Joselyn, particularly because she is his sister. But it just creates a bigger web of obstacles I have to navigate now as I figure out what this crush is.

Is this a crush? Or is this annoyingly charming man just waking up your libido again?

That's the question I still haven't been able to answer. Are my feelings strong just because it's been so long since I've been given male attention and welcomed it? Or is it because the attention is coming from Jeffrey, the type of guy I normally would find maddening and a bit too childish for my tastes.

But he makes me laugh, which is something I haven't done in a long time.

"It's okay to appreciate her body, as long as it's done tastefully."

"Okay. How's this then?" He dips his eyes down to my cleavage for only a second then lifts them back to my eyes. Then he licks his bottom lip, pulls it between his teeth, shaking his head while dragging his thumb across his jaw.

My entire body comes alive, my nipples threatening to slice two holes through the fabric of my dress to make their presence known.

When I haven't said anything for a minute and nothing but my breathing rests between us, Jeffrey breaks the silence. "Too much?"

I clear my throat and grab my next piece in the giant Connect Four game that we're playing on the boardwalk. "Um, no. That was . . . good."

Jeffrey's smile is so blinding it could give fireworks a run for their money as he fist-pumps the air. "Hell, yeah! See, I am learning something."

Yeah, learning how to light the match that's connected to my clit.

I place my red piece in one of the slots and watch it slide down as Jeffrey assesses my move.

The sun is setting in the distance, lighting up the surface of the water of the bay in gold hues that fade to dark blue, hinting at the water beneath. A little breeze rustles through the trees providing shade to us as we play our game, and the bustle of people around us visiting the small shops delivers background noise to our competition.

There's nothing like a summer night in San Diego, and it's been so long since I've genuinely enjoyed one, especially with someone other than my mom.

Jeffrey sighs and drops his yellow piece in one of the slots. "It doesn't matter where I go, you've got me beat, woman."

Shimmying to the board and dropping my final piece in, I do a little victory dance. "That's right, Jeffrey. You've met your match."

He smiles wistfully at me as he shoves his hands in the pockets of his dress pants and tilts his head to the side. "Yeah, I think I have."

Brushing off his endearing comment, I turn around to grab my purse from the ground where I left it while we were playing. It's just a small clutch, but it's big enough for me to carry the essentials and not clash with my outfit.

It's been a long time since this little black dress got a night out on the town, and I forgot how fun it is to wear something other than jeans for once.

"Care to walk around with me?" Jeffrey asks, offering his arm out to me.

"Sure." Looping my arm through his, he sets a slow pace that I can keep up with in my heels as we watch the sun dip down below the horizon.

"I forgot how much I love it down here," he says softly.

"Did you and Joselyn grow up here?"

"Kind of. We lived in Chula Vista, which is about ten miles north of here, but basically still San Diego. My parents always made a point to bring us down to the water as much as they could when we were kids, though. I was obsessed with the boats and playing in the sand like most kids. Joselyn would try to find mermaids in the water and even tried to run into the ocean one time, yelling that she was going to find Ariel." He laughs and then looks at me. "Hey! I guess she finally found you, didn't she?"

I shove his shoulder. "Ha ha. Not funny."

"Oh, come on. I know you said no more Little Mermaid jokes, but that one was too easy."

"Yeah, well, when you've heard them your entire life, they get old."

He stops in his steps, tipping my chin up with his fingers. "I happen to love your name, sweetheart. It fits you so well. You're fiery, driven, and a daydreamer, just like the character was."

I suddenly feel like I'm about to choke on my tongue. "Thank you."

He bops me on the nose. "You're welcome."

Leading me down the sidewalk again, I hold on to him still as I try to remember what we were talking about before. "It would be amazing to grow up here. I can see why people pay to live here now. You're basically paying for the weather."

That makes him laugh. "Yes. Now that I'm in LA, I don't come down here nearly as much, just to see Joselyn and my parents when they're home. But I appreciate how beautiful it is each time."

"Are your parents retired?"

"Yeah, and now they're traveling as much as they want. My dad was in pharmaceutical sales, and my mother was a teacher. They were smart with their money and were able to retire at fifty-seven."

"Any other siblings?" I ask, curious if there are more Davis boys that have the same dimples as Jeffrey. Not that I would be interested in them, but I feel it would be a blessing to the world.

"Nope. Just me and Jos. I think my parents had their hands full with twins, and they got a boy and a girl, so they were content." He eyes me from the side. "What about you? Any siblings?"

Jeffrey might as well have thrown a bucket of water on the flame he was stoking because answering his question would mean having to explain about my dad, and I'm not sure that I want to. I mean, I feel like I can trust Jeffrey with that information, but I haven't opened up to anyone especially a man—about my childhood and how abandoned I felt when he left.

"Um, well . . . I guess I do have siblings, but I don't know them."

His brow furrows. "How does that work?"

"My dad has other kids."

"Oh. So your parents are divorced?"

"Yes." *Let's leave it at that, please.*

"I'm sorry. My parents have been married for over thirty years, and I've always admired what they had. I couldn't imagine having two Christmases and Thanksgivings."

"I don't. My father is not in my life."

"Oh."

"And he never will be."

"Why—"

"How about some ice cream?" I ask, pointing ahead to the shop I see lit up, cutting him off from delving further and suddenly wishing for anything as a distraction from this conversation. The information I just offered Jeffrey was far more than I was willing to in the first place. But there's nothing like a creamy treat to drown yourself in and help you deal with the internal turmoil talking about my childhood dredges up.

The gelato shop on our right has their door propped open, letting out the smell of chocolate and freshly made waffle cones. I grab Jeffrey's hand this time and pull him in that direction, desperate to leave the topic of my father behind.

"Have you been here before?" he asks me as we wait in line.

"No, but I've walked past it. I always try to avoid the temptation."

"Well, this place is one of my favorites. Joselyn and I go here when I'm down for the weekend visiting my parents."

Once we pick our flavors—strawberry cheesecake for Jeffrey and some kind of chocolate concoction with caramel for me—we take our treats to a nearby table and sit, digging in as soon as we can.

"I can't believe you ordered strawberry cheesecake," I say as I dip my spoon into my bowl, lifting up a hefty bite.

"Why?"

"It's just not a very common choice."

"I love fruit in my ice cream." He takes a bite and smiles around his spoon. "There's a flavor at Baskin Robbins called Baseball Nut, and it has swirls of black raspberry and cashews in it. I could eat it every day and not grow tired of it."

I lift my spoon again, sliding the ice cream into my mouth. "That sounds . . ." I go to reply but instantly realize I've made a mistake.

Oh, shit.

"What's wrong?" Jeffrey asks, launching himself from his seat as I drop my spoon on the table and frantically start searching my clutch for my EpiPen.

Oh my God. There has to be hazelnuts in this. Why didn't I read the description closer? I'm usually so good about that.

Shit. This is bad.

"I neeth my EpiPenth," I say as my tongue starts to swell.

"Fuck, Ariel. What's going on?"

My hands are shaking, and I struggle with my clutch until it ultimately slides off my lap just as breathing starts getting difficult. "I neeth my EpiPenth." I clutch my hand around my throat as people start staring in our direction.

Just what I need, a fucking audience.

Jeffrey practically shoves the table away and kneels down on the floor, ripping open my purse. Thank God I had enough sense to put my EpiPen in there before I left. Otherwise, this could have gotten much worse very quickly.

"Tell me what to do," he says as he whips it out.

I reach for it, yanking the blue safety cap straight up from the top and then hiking up the bottom of my dress, exposing my entire right thigh to Jeffrey. But I can't even think about that right now. It's getting harder to breathe with each passing second.

"Holth my handth." I reach for his waiting palm as I inhale as best I can and swing my arm out, landing the Pen hard against my thigh to plunge the needle into my leg.

Jeffrey winces as I count to three in my head and then release the Pen from my thigh, sagging in relief.

"Holy fuck," he says on an exhale.

"Hospital," I croak. "I need to go to the hospital now."

Chapter 9

Jeffrey

"Are you sure she's going to be okay?" I ask the nurse for the hundredth time.

"Yes, hun, I'm sure." The look of irritation she shoots me as she checks Ariel's blood pressure again has me wanting to give her a tongue lashing, but I refrain.

Seeing Ariel start to swell up and struggling to breathe while eating gelato was one of the scariest fucking moments of my life. All I did was hold her hand as she shoved a needle in her leg, but I wish I could have done more. I scooped her up in my arms and ran across the parking lot adjacent to the bay, hoping and praying that she would be all right. I felt so fucking helpless, too, as she groaned in the passenger seat of my car while I rushed her to the emergency room, holding her hand during the entire drive. And you'd best believe I carried her through the automatic doors of the ER like fucking Superman.

And now looking at her lying in the hospital bed with an oxygen mask on her face has me spiraling again.

"I'm okay, Jeffrey," she mumbles behind her mask.

The nurse leaves as I take my seat beside her bed again, hating how small and fragile she still looks. "Just a little PSA, babe . . . you might want to tell your date that you have a severe allergy to hazelnuts ahead of time, just in case something like this happens."

Only the corner of her lips curls, but I see the hint of her smile. "I'm sorry, Jeffrey. I didn't even think about it. And usually I'm so good about being cautious." Her eyes veer off to the side. "I just wasn't thinking straight."

I could tell as soon as I brought up her family, her entire demeanor shifted, which only made me want to dig more. But is that why she wasn't paying attention to the ingredients in the flavor of gelato she chose? Because my questions made her feel off-kilter?

Could part of the reason this woman is so closed off be because of her relationship—or lack thereof—with her dad?

"When did you realize you were allergic to hazelnuts?" I ask her, brushing her hair from her face.

"When I was ten and tried Nutella for the first time. I was so excited, but as soon as I took a bite, I didn't feel right. My tongue swelled, it got hard to breathe, and my skin got hot and itchy. My mother called 911, and we realized quickly that was what it had to be. I've avoided them ever since."

"That sucks. Nutella is the shit."

She lets out a small laugh. "So I've heard." There's a small gap in our conversation before she says, "I want you to know, though, that before this happened, the date was perfect." She squeezes my hand. "I don't think you really need my coaching after all."

I massage her hand right back. "No, this is exactly why I need your help, Ariel," I say, trying not to panic more. "Because of shit like this. This is what happens to me. Although, I will say, I've never had a date have an allergic reaction before. That's a new one."

"Well, you handled the situation perfectly. Passed with flying colors," she teases, giving me a thumbs-up with the hand I'm not holding.

"So, what happens now?"

She releases my hand to pull down her mask so she can talk more easily. "They'll keep me here for a few hours just to monitor me. I can call my mom. She can come wait with me if you want to leave—"

"Not a fucking chance, Ariel," I interrupt her. "I'm not going anywhere. I can call your mom if you want, but I'm not leaving you until I know you're safe at home and another five nurses and doctors tell me you're going to be okay."

She smiles and reaches for my hand again. "I guess there's no use fighting you, then."

"You're damn right. You saw what I can do with a pool ball," I joke. "Imagine what I can do with this television remote." I reach for the remote on the table and swing it around.

She bursts into a fit of giggles, and I take that sound as a win, even though tonight already felt that way before we landed here.

~

"You don't need to come in," Ariel says as she unlocks the front door of her house after one in the morning. The hospital made us stay for four hours before they discharged her.

"I'm gonna make sure you have everything you need, Ariel. I'm not leaving you alone."

"I had an allergic reaction, Jeffrey. I didn't break a bone or hit my head."

"No. This was way worse than that in my opinion." I close the door softly behind us and follow her lead through the dimly lit house. The only light is coming from a night-light in the kitchen.

"Well, I need some water. Are you thirsty?" she whispers, dropping her voice now so as not to wake her mother, I infer.

"Yes, please."

I trail behind her as she makes her way into the kitchen, filling two glasses for us and handing one to me. After we both quench our thirsts, we stare at each other across the space.

The sound of metal clanking rings out, catching her attention from her task. "Are your pants jingling?" she asks when my hips rest against the counter behind me.

"As fun as that would be, no." Huffing out a laugh, she watches me as I dig into my pocket and pull out the handful of change I stuffed in there before I left my apartment. "I was carrying pennies around in case we found a fountain so you could make a wish. I wasn't sure where the evening was going to take us, but I wanted to be prepared."

She stares at me as her jaw drops.

Ariel's face is still a bit swollen, but she looks gorgeous nonetheless. Something about seeing her so vulnerable has only made her dig deeper under my skin. I can tell the reaction took the energy out of her, though. Her eyelids are heavy, and her posture has sunken. Without debating it, I set my glass on the counter, shove the pennies back in my pocket, and stalk across the floor to her, pulling her into my arms.

"I can't believe you did that."

"Well, I brought the lucky ones, too, hoping they would help make your wishes come true, but the evening took an unexpected turn." Shaking my head, I say, "I'm so sorry, Ariel . . . again."

"Stop apologizing. It was my fault."

"I don't think I've ever been so scared in my life."

She pauses before whispering softly, "I was scared, too. But I felt better because you were there. That's pretty stellar date material, I must say."

I tip her chin up so her eyes can meet mine. "Good to know I'm prepared for that in the future now."

"Yeah. That's one lucky girl."

We stand there in a stare-off, waiting for the other to say something else, but all I can focus on is how hard my heart is pounding while holding her in my arms, how desperately I want to press my lips to hers.

But is that what she wants? I know she just had an allergic reaction, so maybe the thought of a kiss right now isn't the best idea.

Christ, do I want to kiss her, though.

Instead, I settle on pressing my lips to her forehead, listening to her breathe in deeply as I clutch her to my chest.

"Ariel?" The sound of her mother racing into the kitchen has us retreating from our stance, acting like two teenagers who just got caught.

"Hey, Mom."

The woman who looks like an older version of the one who was just in my arms reaches out for her, pulling her in for a hug. "Oh, honey. Are you okay?"

"Yes. I'm fine. I told you I was."

After the nurses told us they were going to monitor her for a while, Ariel called her mom. She wanted to come down to the hospital, but Ariel told her that by the time she got there, they'd be sending her home. It wasn't the entire truth, but she told me she didn't want to make her mom drive all the way there. And then she explained that she wasn't alone, which led to me talking to the woman standing in front of me, reassuring her that I was taking care of her daughter.

Ariel's mom turns to me at that moment. "You must be

Jeffrey." She extends a hand toward me while keeping the other one wrapped around Ariel.

"Yes, ma'am. It's nice to meet you."

"Catherine. You can call me Catherine, honey." She releases Ariel and then rushes toward me, hugging me tightly. I look over her shoulder at Ariel, my eyes bugging out while Ariel fights her laughter. "Thank you for taking care of my girl."

Hugging her back, I say, "It was my pleasure. I wish there was more I could have done."

"I know the feeling." She unwraps her arms from me, grasping my shoulder. "I hate when she has a reaction, although it hasn't happened in a long time."

"I told you—I was distracted," Ariel says, glaring at the ground.

That has her mother looking between the two of us, one of her brows raised. "I see. Well, Jeffrey, I can't thank you enough. I'll leave you two alone, but I just had to make sure that my girl was okay."

"I'm fine, Mom. I'll see you in the morning."

"Love you, honey." Catherine kisses Ariel's temple and then squeezes my forearm as she passes me. "Thank you again, Jeffrey."

"Of course. I'd do it again in a heartbeat." I watch her leave and head back down the hall just as Ariel folds her arms over her chest. "Your mom seems nice."

"Yes. And meddlesome."

I smirk at her irritation. Perhaps Mother Dearest senses the connection between us that Ariel so blatantly wants to ignore. Or maybe finding us in the position we were in before she interrupted has her curious as well.

Pulling Ariel back in my arms again, I say, "Most moms are. Hey, I don't want this to sound forward, but do you mind if I sleep on your couch?"

She rears back to meet my gaze again. "What?"

"It's too late to drive back to Joselyn's place. I don't want to wake her. And I'm exhausted. Plus, I really don't want to leave you."

Something flashes through her eyes, shock mixed with reverence. "Yeah, I guess that makes sense."

"And normally I sleep in my underwear, but I promise, I'll remain fully clothed." I hold up two fingers in the Boy Scout salute.

She chuckles and then pushes herself out of my hold. "Probably best that way. If my mother wakes up and finds a nearly naked man on our couch, the interrogation that will ensue won't ever end."

"Your mom won't mind, will she?"

"No. I'll explain everything to her later." She takes one more drink of her water. "Let me go get you some blankets."

I move to the living room to take off my shoes and fluff the pillows on the couch. I'm not a giant man, but sleeping here is going to be challenging and will probably hurt for a few days after. I don't care, though. I want to be here in case Ariel needs me. The doctor said that side effects can last up to ten days after an attack, and if she's alone and her mother doesn't hear her, who the hell knows how quickly things could turn?

"Here you go." Ariel comes down the hallway ten minutes later dressed in tiny silk shorts and a matching cami in a deep navy color. From what I can see in the dark, it looks like she's not wearing a bra, either, which is probably true given the way her nipples are standing at attention right now.

Fuck. This is what she sleeps in?

"Uh, thanks." I grab the blanket and pillow from her and just stand there, wondering what else to say. "I like your pajamas." *Jesus. That is what you decide?*

"Thank you."

"They're very shiny."

Ariel raises a brow. "They are."

"And blue."

She rolls her eyes at me and then steps forward, planting her lips on my cheek. And in that moment, I'm grateful that she doesn't come too much closer, otherwise my dick will be poking her in the stomach.

You cannot jack off on her couch, dude. Don't even think about it.

I wasn't!

Yes, you were. Save the image of her in this little outfit for later. It will be worth it.

"Goodnight, Jeffrey."

"Goodnight, Ariel."

She turns to walk away from me but pauses and looks back over her shoulder. "Thanks for being such a good friend."

As if she just stabbed me through the heart, I fall back on the couch, groaning as I drag my hands down my face while I hear her bedroom door softly shut.

Suddenly, I feel like I'm in way over my head here, which means I'm the one who stands to get hurt—just like every time before.

~

Scratching my balls like I do every morning, I feel my morning wood standing at attention. My eyes are still closed, but the vision of Ariel in her silk pajamas comes rushing back as I fight the urge to give myself a proper wake-up call.

And that's when last night slams back into me.

I launch myself up so I'm sitting on the couch, scanning the room in a panic.

I'm in Ariel's house, and I was just stroking my dick and scratching my balls through my pants. Fuck, that could have been bad.

Luckily, I didn't have an audience for my little rubdown, so I lean back and take a few deep breaths to get my heart rate back to normal.

"Well, good morning."

I shriek like a little girl, jumping up from the couch, spinning to face the owner of the voice that just took five years off my life.

Ariel's mom stares back at me, wearing a sundress like she's already dressed for the day, and looking into her knowing eyes is like staring at the girl I'm crushing on but twenty years down the road.

"Um, hello."

Catherine lifts her coffee mug to her lips, smiling around the rim before taking a sip. "It's not every day that I wake up to a strange man sleeping on my couch. In fact, I can't say that this has ever happened before at all."

"Well, there's always a first time for everything."

Her grin builds. "Yes, there is."

"Sorry. I hope you don't mind. I was beat after last night and didn't want to leave Ariel by herself."

"She wasn't by herself."

"I know." Shoving my hands in my pockets, I wait for her reaction. She grins around the lip of her mug again. "But the doctor said that the reaction could linger, and I wanted to make sure she didn't have any issues. I even set an alarm on my phone every hour to check on her."

And I did. Even though it made for one of the shittiest nights of sleep in my life, I made sure she was still breathing and resting, every hour on the hour.

"What a good . . . *friend*," she emphasizes as she glances down the hallway where Ariel's bedroom door is still shut. "But something tells me you wish you were more."

I huff out a laugh. "Am I that obvious?"

"It's not about being obvious, Jeffrey. It's about your actions. Any other guy might not have reacted the way you did when Ariel had her attack. How you supported her through that and even after speaks a lot about the man you are."

"That's the type of man I want to be, Catherine. Unfortunately, in my life, the cliché that 'nice guys finish last' has proven true."

"Yeah, but they still finish." She winks at me. "Be patient with my daughter, Jeffrey. She doesn't trust easily, with good reason. But I know the right man can make her see that risking her heart can be worth it."

"Thank you, Catherine. I really want to be that man for her."

"Something tells me you already are. And being her friend is a great first step."

"I've gotten pretty good at being the friend," I joke. And as much as it kills me to classify myself that way, I feel that it's probably safer than lying to her mom about us dating or trying to explain that I'm using a ruse to get to know Ariel. Knowing how pissed off she was when I revealed our arrangement to my sister, the last thing I want to do is make the same mistake with her mom—at least until we can discuss it.

See? My training is working.

"Oh my God!" Ariel comes tripping over herself down the hallway, wrapping a robe around her body. "Mom. Sorry I didn't tell you, but—"

"—Jeffrey stayed the night," her mom finishes for her. "I kind of gathered that when I woke up and heard him snoring on the couch."

With wild bed hair and wide eyes, Ariel looks so fucking cute right now. I wish I could drag her back to her bed and make her hair even messier than it already is. But the panic on her face tells me that she was hoping she could have prevented the moment when her mother would wake and find me on the couch.

That probably would have been better than whatever this is.

At least my morning wood faded rather quickly after being scared shitless just a few moments ago.

Brushing her hair from her face, Ariel wraps her arms around her body. "Yes. Jeffrey was exhausted, and it was late, so I suggested he stay on the couch so he didn't have to drive home." Pretty sure I asked to stay, but I concede it sounds better as Ariel's idea.

I raise my hand in the air. "And I appreciate the hospitality. Your couch was lovely to sleep on, Catherine. Truly." The crick in my neck says otherwise, but I'm trying to win over this woman right now.

"I appreciate you being kind, but I know what a night of sleep on that couch feels like. I recommend a full body massage to recover."

I crack my neck from side to side. "Yeah, that might be necessary."

Catherine looks between the two of us, her eyes bouncing back and forth rapidly, her smile growing just as fast. "Well, I best be going. The grocery store gets crowded if I get there after ten on a Sunday." Setting her coffee cup on the kitchen counter, she turns back to us. "It was so nice to meet you, Jeffrey. Thanks again for taking care of Ariel and being such a good . . . *friend* to her."

She passes by me, planting a kiss on my cheek and then doing the same to her daughter, grabbing her purse before waving and walking out the front door.

"Oh God, I'm never going to hear the end of that." Ariel groans, moving toward the kitchen and pulling a coffee mug from the cupboard.

"Sorry. I wanted to be awake so she wasn't caught off guard. But I was exhausted and didn't even hear her."

She spins to face me. "Did you really wake up every hour to check on me last night?" Her question comes out as almost a whisper, but I can hear the hope in her voice.

"I did. Did you hear us talking?"

"Vaguely. Your voices are what woke me up, and that's what I heard first." I watch her swallow hard and then turn around again, setting the mug on the counter before facing me once more. She looks perfect, like last night didn't even happen. Her face has returned to normal, her lips are bare but still enticing, and her nipples are standing at attention under her robe through her cami. "You know, our date ended so abruptly that we didn't get a chance to talk about how to properly end it," she says, waking me up more than coffee would or her mother scaring the shit out of me did earlier.

"You're right."

She takes a few steps toward me. "So if my allergic reaction hadn't happened, would you have kissed me? I mean, if I was your real date?"

This conversation just took a turn that I will gladly follow. "Do you think I should have?"

"Only if you think that's what your date wanted."

"I think that's what *you* wanted, you know . . . if you were *actually* my date."

She bites her bottom lip. "Well, maybe we should practice, you know . . . for research purposes."

"Are you sure?"

She nods, wrapping her arms around my neck. "Confidence is key, Jeffrey. Kiss me like you mean it."

I do mean it, I want to say. But instead, I inhale deeply and move my mouth toward hers, waiting with bated breath for our lips to touch.

And when they do, I know there's nothing better than the feeling of Ariel's mouth and body pressed up against mine. I've officially died and gone to heaven.

I kiss her with intent, demanding and hard with a sense of urgency, like if I don't kiss her now, I may never get the chance to. I drag my tongue over hers with reverence, like I'm trying to create a melody with our mouths. I pull her tightly to my chest, pressing our torsos together so she can feel what she's doing to me.

Her moans of pleasure urge me on as I back her up against the counter, pressing my cock right between the juncture of her legs. She rakes her fingers over the stubble on my jaw, trembling as I nibble on her bottom lip.

We become entranced in each other, forgetting the boundaries that we drew in the beginning and stepping over them so far that I know there's no going back for me now. Meeting this woman was kismet. Spending time with her has quickly become my obsession.

And kissing her is so damn electric that I'm surprised I'm not suffering from shock right now.

When air becomes scarce and I can feel myself on the border of losing control, I slow down the pace, memorizing the shape and taste of her mouth before pulling back and filling my lungs with much-needed air.

Ariel's eyes slowly lift and meet mine, but I can't read her. Was that too much? Did I take it too far?

She said to be confident, and that kiss was every ounce of desire I've had for this woman since the moment I met her bundled up in a package that is getting harder and harder to contain with every moment we spend together.

"How was that?" I grate out, my voice sounding like gravel, my cock still hard as steel.

"That was good . . ." She inhales deeply. "Nice."

"Just *nice*?"

She bites her bottom lip. "Yeah. *Really* nice."

Fuck, we've got to work on this girl's adjectives once we make this relationship real. Although, if the only word she can think of is *nice*, then I guess I melted her brain to mush, which is a compliment in itself.

Gotta look for the silver lining here.

"Care to make it great?" I challenge, leaning in to capture her lips again. But she stops me, holding her hand up. I laugh behind her palm.

"Um, that's not necessary. You've proven that first kisses aren't something you need to worry about."

Hell, yes. The student is becoming the master.

Although, I never really doubted my kissing skills. Even when it comes to sex, I'm a fast learner. I have no problem asking a woman what she needs or how I can make her come. In fact, I prefer it that way. You'd be surprised how many girls are shocked when I do ask and say that most men don't.

We've got to do better, guys.

"One less thing to coach me on then, huh?" I say, fighting my smile.

"Yup." Ariel walks away from me now, almost tripping over the rug. "Jesus! When did that get there?" She spins around and pushes her hair from her face, her eyes flitting around the room, avoiding meeting mine. Her cheeks are flushed, her nipples are fully erect, and I swear I can see her clenching her thighs together.

I'm having the best time watching her freak-out occur before my eyes, even though I'm pretty sure the kiss was her idea. But before she goes too far and slips back into defense mode, I'd better give her some space.

Jutting my thumb over my shoulder, I say, "Listen, I'd best be going. I still need to swing by Joselyn's to grab my stuff and drive home. I've got a couple of errands I need to run before work tomorrow, too, so I'll get out of your hair."

"Oh. Okay. Yeah, sounds good."

"I'll call you, and we can make plans next weekend?"

She nods overenthusiastically. And all her nerves make me want to do is kiss her again. Fuck, she's cute like this. "Sure."

"Have a good day, Ariel. Thanks for an unforgettable night."

With one quick press of my lips to her cheek, I grab my wallet and keys from the table by the door and let myself out, skipping down the driveway to my car. I'm feeling like, despite everything that happened with Ariel's reaction, I just experienced one of the best dates and mornings of my life.

Chapter 10

Ariel

"Stupid rugs." Nearly falling flat on my face for the third time today, I kick the rubber mat lying in one of the halls between the dressing rooms and the set of *Joselyn and Hunter in the Morning*. Yeah, they've officially changed the name of the show.

But in the past three weeks, that's not the only thing that's changed.

Somehow, I've gone from the girl who wants nothing to do with men to a woman who can only think of *one* man, a man I'm supposed to be coaching on dating but have ultimately ended up dating myself.

Jesus, how the hell did this happen?

It's been more than twenty-four hours since Jeffrey left my

house, and I can still feel his lips pressed against mine. In fact, I think that kiss was one of the best I've had in my entire life. I don't have much to compare it to, but it's easy to tell the difference between a mediocre kiss and one that you feel all the way down to the tips of your toes.

And I asked for it—that's the kicker.

After hearing Jeffrey tell my mother that he woke up throughout the night to check on me, multiple walls crumbled around my heart.

What kind of guy does that?

The kind that might be on his best behavior in the beginning just to pull the rug out from under you later, just like your ex did—and your dad.

But the thing is—my gut tells me he's not. That the man I get when I'm with Jeffrey is exactly who he is. Jeffrey doesn't hide, he's honest—even though sometimes he's a little *too* honest—and he's genuine. His easygoing nature is infectious. Hell, being with him has even reminded me to be more relaxed and go with the flow, which is just what he said he could do for me.

So why am I questioning this?

Well, part of it has to do with the woman standing in front of me, the one with crossed arms over her chest and an arched eyebrow as if she was waiting for me to enter her office just now.

I close the door behind me and prepare for the conversation I've been dreading all weekend.

Raising my voice an octave, I say, "Hey, Jos. Great show today! Seems you and Hunter are starting to vibe a little bit better."

"We're . . . starting to come to an agreement in our working relationship," she replies, her eyes darting away for a second before returning to my own. And then she goes straight for the jugular. "So, you're coaching my brother?"

"Uh, yeah?" It comes out more as a question than a definitive answer as I move further into the room.

"Care to elaborate? Because the last time we spoke of Jeffrey, you said he wasn't your type and you two were better off friends."

"We are. He asked me out, I turned him down, and then he asked me to help him with the ladies, so . . . I am," I reply so nonchalantly that I'm even convincing myself it's not that big of a deal.

"Are you sure that's all this is, Ariel? I . . . I don't want to see my brother get hurt." She drops her hands and then motions toward the couch for us to sit down.

Letting out a heavy sigh, I relent and plop down onto the cushions, staring up at the ceiling. "Joselyn . . . I have no idea what I'm doing."

She props her head up in one of her hands, her arm resting on the back of the couch. "I kind of figured as much. Talk to me about it. I promise, I'll remain neutral."

Knowing I need to talk to someone about my confusion, I relent, sinking further into the couch. "Your brother seemed so excited about the idea that I sort of caved when he asked me to help him. But the more time I spend with him—"

"—the further he gets under your skin," she finishes for me.

"Yes." Turning my head to face her, I continue. "And the man doesn't need help in the dating department. In fact, despite all the obstacles we've encountered . . ." I take a minute to tell her about the pool ball to the toe, the foot to the nose, and the allergic reaction incident. ". . . he's proven that his heart is pure. We were even able to laugh about it after the fact."

Joselyn smiles knowingly. "That's Jeffrey."

"And then he kissed me . . ."

"He did?"

"I kind of asked for it."

Playfully, she shoves my shoulder. "Who are you?"

Chuckling, I throw my hands up in the air. "I don't even know. But God, Jos, the man can kiss."

She holds her hand up. "Listen, I'm glad it did something for you, but please remember, I don't need details about my brother's"—she grimaces—"skills."

Laughing, I nod. "Fine."

"In all honesty, I thought maybe more had happened between the two of you when he didn't come home Saturday night."

"Uh, no. I was not about to go there yet."

"Yet?" She grins, bouncing her eyebrows.

"Jesus. What are you, twelve? You're acting like your brother right now!"

She tosses her head back as she laughs. "Okay. I'm sorry. Go on."

"It was just so late by the time we got home from the hospital Saturday night that he slept on the couch. And then he checked on me throughout the night." I sigh wistfully. "That was what sealed it for me—the notion that maybe he's worth risking my no-man ban." And then I groan. "But the last thing I wanted was to date, and yet here I am dating your brother under unusual circumstances, and now I'm not sure that I want him to date other women. I think . . . I think I want him to date me."

She claps her hands together rapidly. "Oh my God!"

"Calm down." I bat at her hands. "I'm still terrified, though."

"Why?"

I bite my lip, contemplating opening up about my fear of letting people in. But I know Joselyn. I know she won't judge me. Even though I've only been her assistant for a few months, we have a connection, a friendship, so I know that I can trust her. "Because trusting people has not panned out well for me in the past. My father . . . he had an affair behind my mother's back for years, building a family with two other children that we had no idea about." God, it feels surreal to say that out loud to another person.

She gasps. "Holy shit, Ariel."

"I was ten, and my brother and sister, whom I never knew existed, were eight and six. You do the math." Grinding my teeth together, I suppress the anger I keep reserved just for him.

"That's his loss, Ariel. You shouldn't have to pay for his mistakes, and you shouldn't make other people pay for them, either."

"I know, but it's hard to articulate. If the man who was supposed to be in my life unconditionally could leave with a snap of my fingers—and he did once my mom found out—why wouldn't any other person do that, too? Not to mention that my latest ex, whom I dated for a year, was cheating on me the entire time." I take a moment to recall the devastation that Joey left in his wake. "He said all the right things, made me think I was everything he wanted, and then I discovered his Tinder profile. When he was in the shower one day, I went through his phone and found so many messages and pictures from girls, it made me vomit. I was completely blindsided, and I swore to myself that I would never feel that way again."

"Do you think Jeffrey would do that to you, though?" she asks genuinely, but my answer probably isn't what she wants to hear.

"I don't know, Jos. I honestly don't know because as amazing as he seems—and I'm not just saying that because he's your brother—I'm beginning to wonder if . . ." My voice cracks, and my eyes sting with tears as I contemplate voicing my worst fear.

She reaches out and squeezes my hand. "What, hun?"

". . . if I'm the problem," I whisper, letting a tear slide down my cheek, quickly batting it away. "What if it's me, Jos? What if at some point I'm doing or saying something that is pushing these men out of my life?"

She stares at me, turning her lips in on themselves before she speaks. "Ariel . . ." Taking a deep breath, she says, "First of all, I'm so sorry that these things have happened to you. I can't imagine feeling that kind of betrayal, especially from a father. But I think it's important to realize that your relationship with your father is different than your relationship with a man you're trying to date. The thing with your dad was about him and his shortcomings, not you. You and your mother didn't do anything wrong."

"That's what my mother tried to tell me, too."

"Well, she sounds like a smart woman." Winking at me, she smiles and then speaks once more. "And the thing with your ex? Well, some men just don't have the capacity for monogamy. They don't have the ability to be intimate with one person. And I'm not talking about just sexually. I mean real intimacy. Being vulnerable with one person. I truly think that's why men cheat and we as women turn the problem around on us. I wish more men were emotionally mature or weren't so afraid to be in tune with their emotions. It would save us all a lot of heartache." She tilts her head at me and lowers her voice. "But you were never going to be able to break through his shortcomings, hun, and again—that's his problem, not yours."

I grip her hand tighter. "I appreciate that. But it still doesn't change the fact that betrayal like that leaves scars."

"I wish more people understood how powerful their words and actions can be toward another human being, their power to scar us on a level so far beneath the surface that it makes breathing seem difficult."

"You sound like you're speaking from experience."

"You're not the only one with a scumbag ex, honey." She arches a brow at me. "But I promised myself that I would never let a man hold that kind of power over me, to change how I view love or to not be willing to give my heart away again. I don't want to give someone and their actions that kind of hold over my happiness."

Breathing out, I say, "Wow. You make it sound so simple."

"It's not. I struggle with it every day . . . even now, actually."

"What do you mean?"

She bites her lip, wincing. "I kissed Hunter on Friday."

That has me jolting up in my seat. "What? How? Why?"

"Oh God." She puts her face in her hands. "I can't get into this right now, okay? This is about you, remember?"

I narrow my eyes at her. "Fine, but we are going to revisit that little revelation soon."

"There will be nothing more to speak about. It was a moment of weakness, and he hasn't even mentioned it since."

"See? Men are jerks."

"Yes, some men are, but Jeffrey is not," she says, bringing our conversation back to the man in question. "And if he's making you even contemplate letting someone in again, I'd say that speaks volumes. I know your agreement is fuzzy and growing fuzzier by the moment, but I say you go for it. See it through, and then maybe, at the end, you tell him how you feel." She shrugs. "What's the worst that could happen?"

"I don't even want to answer that question," I whisper.

"Look, no matter what happens, I promise I won't let it affect our working relationship or friendship, okay?"

"Promise? Because I would hate for awkwardness every time he came to visit you. Or for you to hate me down the road . . ."

"Let's just cross that bridge if we get to it, all right?"

I blow out a harsh breath. "Okay."

"So keep doing what you're doing, assess your feelings as they arise, and hopefully at one point, you'll come to a decision about what you want. You're only twenty-five. You're too young to be this jaded about love."

Laughing, I reply, "I think I can do that." At least, I hope I can. The more I think about it, the more I want to. I want to believe Jeffrey won't hurt me. I want to chase this high he makes me feel. And even more than all that, perhaps most importantly, he allows me to be myself—to laugh and smile and not hide or feel I need to be someone I'm not.

"Good." She stands from the couch, headed for her vanity. "Now—"

"Wait! What about the thing with Hunter?"

She sighs, leaning her head back to stare at the ceiling. "Girl . . . that's a story that doesn't have an ending yet."

"What is he doing?" I'm currently sitting in my room, watching Jeffrey on our doorbell camera, fidgeting on our front porch. He's pacing back and forth, adjusting his pants from behind.

Wait . . . is he picking his wedgie?

"Oh my God." Covering my mouth with my hand to stifle my laughter, I watch him squirm and readjust himself for a few more minutes before I decide to put him out of his misery.

"Finally. I was wondering how long you were going to leave him out there," my mother says as I come down the hallway.

"Well, technically, he hasn't rung the doorbell yet."

"True. Where are you two headed tonight?"

"I'm not sure, actually. He told me to dress comfortably, so I did." I look down at my cut-off jean shorts, pink tank top, and tan wedges. I also have a caramel-colored cardigan in my hands in case it gets colder later, since it always does once the sun goes down and the breeze comes in off the water in the bay.

"Well, I hope you have an amazing time." My mother walks up to me and kisses me on the forehead. "Whatever is happening between you and him, I support it. I've never seen you smile this much." And then she walks to her room, leaving me standing there, rattling my nerves even more.

After my talk with Joselyn on Monday, I knew that she was right. I had to continue this ruse so I could make sure that dating Jeffrey was what I truly wanted. And the more I thought about it, the more it helped ease my discomfort. Somehow the notion that this isn't exactly real dating helps lessen the pressure. And I wouldn't say that I'm necessarily leading him on since he thinks this is fake, too, so no harm if, at the end, we part ways just as we agreed.

But this week, he gave me a reminder of what it's like to be interested in someone and want to hear from them every day. Throughout the week, he texted me on and off—asking how my morning was, whether I had encountered any hazelnuts at all, and if I managed to read my book that he purchased for me, which I finally did start last Sunday.

We communicated back and forth without pressure to say the right thing. I didn't contemplate every text I sent or wonder what he was doing if he didn't respond right away. In fact, he was very diligent about telling me that he couldn't really respond during certain times of the day because of work. And the gym selfie he sent me one evening may have served as some spank bank material that night.

In all honesty, the physical aspect of dating again is the part I'm least concerned about, especially after our kiss in my kitchen. It's been so long since I've been touched that I know I won't mind if our arrangement gravitates to those types of lessons one bit.

Ironically, Joselyn called me out several times when she caught me grinning down at my phone at work, lost in conversation with him. But other than that, she didn't press me any further about my feelings, which I appreciated. I think she and I said all that we needed to say on Monday about the situation, so now the ball is in my court.

Let's just hope I figure out what to do with it.

I move toward the door just as Jeffrey finally rings the doorbell. Waiting a few moments before answering, I pull open the door and find him standing there, grinning like the Cheshire cat.

"Hey, babe."

For once, I don't want to tell him that I'm not his *babe*. So I don't, because now I kind of like the way it sounds. "Hi, Jeffrey."

His eyes dip down my body and then back up. "You look beautiful."

"You said comfortable, so this is what I went with. Will it be okay?"

"Absolutely."

"You looked a little *uncomfortable* there for a moment," I say, teasing him as I lean against the doorframe.

"What do you mean?"

I hold up my phone in my hand and then point it toward the doorbell camera. "I was watching you. Took you long enough to finally let me know you were here."

His face falls. "Oh. You, uh, saw that, huh?"

"Yup. Had a wedgie there, did ya?" I can't help smiling at the awkwardness on his face.

But then he takes a deep breath, puffs out his chest, and emits an air of confidence. "I could be embarrassed that you caught that, or I could just own up to it. So I will. Yes, Ariel, I was picking my underwear out of my butt cheeks. It's actually a very common problem, so I'm not sure why people feel the need to make a big fuss about it."

Giggling, I lean my head against the doorframe now. "Wow. Just putting it all out there, huh?"

"I mean, why try to hide it? We all encounter that situation from time to time. It would be like trying to cover up a fart if you clearly heard it." My eyes go wide. "We all do it, so why is it such a big deal? I mean, if you farted in front of me, I wouldn't make you feel bad about it. In fact, I think it signals a level of comfort with one another."

Mortified now, I push off the doorframe, grab my purse, and shut the door behind me, joining him on the front step. "Uh, I will *not* be farting in front of you anytime soon, Jeffrey, okay?"

His mischievous grin makes its appearance. "Why not? I think you'd have the cutest little toots of any girl I've ever met."

I spin around and smack his chest. "Oh my God! Don't say toots!"

"Is that your advice as my dating coach?"

"That's my advice as a woman! Don't talk about her farts with her, okay?"

He holds his stomach, his head dropping back as he laughs out loud. "Okay. No more fart talk. But in my defense, you brought it up by pointing out my wedgie predicament."

"That's different."

"Hmm, I don't think so. They both involve butts."

Shaking my head at him, we head for his car. He opens the door for me, allowing me to buckle before shutting it and rounding the front of his car to his side, situating himself before heading to our destination of the night.

We make small talk on the way there, catching each other up on our week, details we didn't talk about through our text messages. And as we cruise toward the harbor, I can feel myself relax, even though the anticipation of where he's taking me is building as we get closer to the water.

When Jeffrey parks the car, he turns to face me. "Have you ever been on a cruise around the harbor?"

"No..."

"Well, then, I'd love for you to join me." He holds his hand out to me.

I rest mine in his palm. "Okay."

"Before we board the boat, though, I need to know if you get seasick . . . if so, I did bring some Dramamine."

"Oh my gosh . . ." I giggle, internally swooning at how sweet and thoughtful he is.

"And all I ask is that you don't get too close to the railing of the boat. The last thing we need is another disaster on our date. I don't want to have to jump in the ocean after you if you fall over. I will, but I'd rather we try to get through this date with no bodily injury or hospital visits."

Laughing, I lean over the center console and press my lips to his, surprising us both. His eyes are wide as he stares back at me. "I think we can do that. I have faith in us."

Smirking, Jeffrey exits the car and opens my door, offering his hand to help me up. Once he locks the car, he grabs my hand and leads us to the dock where people are in line, waiting to board. The wooden slats creak beneath our feet, seagulls fly over our heads, and the salty breeze assaults my senses.

I've heard of these dinner cruises, but I've never gone on one myself.

But I'm glad I get to experience it with Jeffrey, even if things between us don't progress beyond our arrangement.

That's a possibility I still need to consider. On top of the fact that just because I might want more from him doesn't mean he'll want me back.

Chapter 11

Jeffrey

"What is something everyone else likes but you don't?" I spear my fork through another piece of lobster and deposit it into my mouth, waiting for Ariel to answer.

As soon as we boarded the boat, Ariel insisted we stay on the deck as we took off into the bay. She clutched onto the railing to get the best view, but I was serious about making sure nothing happened to her again, so I stood behind her, flanking her with my own hands gripping the railing beside hers. The close proximity allowed me to breathe her in without seeming like a creep, but the closeness was everything I wanted out of this evening—especially the smile on her face as our boat coasted through the water and she took in the scenery.

That smile was worth every penny and every ounce of effort I've invested in this woman so far.

Now, we're seated at our table on the deck, the sun setting behind us as we devour the main course of our four-course meal. I made sure to triple-check our food had no trace of hazelnuts in or near it. The crew assured me there weren't even hazelnuts on board the ship, which helped me relax a bit more.

And even though the coast is behind her, highlighting everything there is to love about San Diego, I can only stare at her.

Her skin is glowing from the rays of the sun, her eyes look even lighter—the flecks of gold in them are highlighted more than normal in the light—and her smile is captivating me more than ever. Especially her lips.

God, do I want to taste those again.

"Do you mean food-wise?"

"Sure. Or anything, really. I want to know your dislikes. I find those more telling than what you do enjoy."

"Interesting." She contemplates her answer, dabbing at her mouth with her napkin. "Well, I really hate Styrofoam containers."

"Styrofoam containers?"

"Yup. Not only are they terrible for the planet, but the way they feel and the sound they make . . ." She shudders. "It freaks me out."

Chuckling, I say, "Okay. What else?"

"Oh! Hiccups! I think they are so annoying."

"Agreed."

"And socks. I can't stand them. They get in between my toes. They make my feet sweat. And if the line on the top is off-center, I want to scream."

Tossing my head back, I let out a jovial laugh. "Kind of sounds like how I feel about wedgies."

She narrows her eyes at me. "You're really going to bring that up again?"

"Couldn't resist." I wink at her. "Okay, what about things you *do* like? Or something that makes you feel at peace?"

"Hmm." She taps her finger to her chin. "Well, the color blue always makes me feel calm and content. I could stare at the sky and clouds all day."

"Okay . . ."

"And when the seasons change and you can leave the windows open at night when you sleep . . . like that crisp air that hits your skin and feels so refreshing." She sighs. "That's the best."

"Oh, that's a good one."

"And nachos. I could eat nachos every day."

Her last one makes me smile. "Good to know."

She grabs her glass of wine, swirling around the liquid before lifting it to her lips. "What about you, Jeffrey? I can't be the only one to share that stuff."

I shift my body weight in my seat. "All right. Well, dislikes first, then?"

She nods. "Yes."

"I hate hangnails. I think they're one of the worst boo-boos you can get."

"Did you just say 'boo-boos'?"

"Yes, I did, babe. Because that's what they are."

She giggles. "Okay . . . continue, please."

"I can't stand golf . . . like everything about it. I think it's the most boring sport ever."

"I agree with you on that one."

"And food-wise? I'd have to say cold French fries. There is nothing worse than ordering a fast-food meal and getting cold, soggy fries."

"Oh! That's a good one. Definite pet peeve of mine." Ariel's eyes grow wide as she takes a sip of her wine. "Okay, your likes."

"I love thunderstorms, especially when I can watch them from inside my house."

"Oh, yes. I love that, too."

"I love my friends. They are like family to me. Damien and his entire crew . . . they've welcomed me in even though I'm kind of the odd one out. But they make me feel like I'm a part of something real. They're the kind of people I know would be there for me if I needed them, and it took me a long time to find that in life, so I try to cherish that."

Her face softens. "That's amazing, Jeffrey."

"And last . . . I love the idea of love." Her lips part, but I want her to know where I stand with this. "I am so ready to find that one person in my life I can't get enough of, the one person who I want to dedicate my time and thoughts to. I want to find someone who's my best friend but also accepts me for who I am and everything I have to offer." Shrugging, I keep my eyes locked on hers. "Call me a romantic, but it's all I've ever really wanted in my life. Sometimes I wonder if it will happen."

Ariel's eyes gloss over before she stands from her seat, comes over to mine, and situates herself on my lap. She brushes my hair from my face and stares down into my eyes as I wrap my arms around her, holding her safely in place. "It will happen, Jeffrey. I don't know why it hasn't yet, but—"

"I've just been waiting for the right person." I cup her jaw. "That's why I wanted your help, Ariel. I want to find her."

"I think she might want to be found, too."

Our lips meet with no hesitation, and suddenly the rockiness of the waves has nothing on the smooth cadence of the beat of my heart. Ariel's soft mouth molds to my own as I dart my tongue out to find hers.

We get lost in our kiss, oblivious to the other people on the boat. I'm pretty sure a waiter comes by at one point to clear our plates, but I don't dare pull away from Ariel when she's offering herself to me like this.

Part of me wonders if she even knows that she's doing it. Is she acting on instinct? Is kissing me deliberate? Or is she so absorbed in her role of my fake date that she wants the lesson to feel as real as possible?

Either way, I'm not complaining. And part of me thinks that the woman in my arms right now, the woman who's been opening herself up to me over the past three weeks, is genuinely her. Perhaps she's starting to feel what I felt the first day I met her: an undeniable attraction and connection that means I'm not destined to just be this woman's friend.

That just maybe I can be more to her.

With one more soft press of my mouth to hers, I break our kiss and lean back, waiting for her eyes to meet mine.

"Jeffrey—"

She gets cut off by the captain's voice over the sound system. "Ladies and gentlemen, as the dinner service wraps up, we ask that you start making your way toward the deck to partake in the tour of San Diego's coast and remarkable landmarks."

Ariel stands from my lap, fixing the hair my hands were just wrapped up in, her demeanor far less confident than she was when she initiated that kiss. In fact, she looks rather frazzled and confused, and I'm not sure that's a good thing. "Um, I'm going to run to the restroom really quick before the tour starts."

"Okay. I'll be here." Watching her walk away, I adjust myself in my pants and gulp down my glass of water.

I'm not sure what's happening, but I don't have time to question it. I just want to see the night through and use every moment together to prove I am the right man for her.

And if that kiss was any indication, I'd say I'm getting closer to achieving that goal.

∼

"All right. On a scale from one to ten, how'd I do, Coach?" I'm driving back to Ariel's house after our cruise ended.

And even though it feels better to be back on land, I can't deny that holding her in my arms as the sky turned dark and we marveled at all the lights of the city around us was one of my favorite parts of the evening.

Besides that kiss.

That moment takes the cake.

"Eh, I'd say a solid eight."

"What?" I cast a glance at her before focusing back on the road. But I can see the uptick of her smile. "That's like getting a B. I don't accept that. How do I make it an A?"

"Well, we'll see how you do when you drop me off," she tosses back at me playfully. "Although, I have to say that was an experience I'll never forget. I've lived here most of my life and have never done that. It's amazing how you can appreciate your surroundings just from a different view."

"I get that. Is there anything else you've never experienced here that you really want to?"

She ponders for a moment. "I know this might sound silly, but San Diego is known for some remarkable spa resorts. I've never been to one. I've always wanted to take my mom and spend the day pampering ourselves, but we could never afford it. Or life just kind of got in the way."

"That's not silly at all. Perhaps you can make that happen for the two of you soon."

"Yeah, I think I need to. You only live once, you know?"

Her words hit me square in the chest, reminding me of the chance I'm taking on her. And the longer this goes on, the more I need to decide just how to cross that line between her helping me and me trying to date her for real.

A few minutes later, we arrive at her house. After I cut the engine and help her out of the car, I place my hand on the small of her back as we make our way up her driveway to her porch. When she spins to face me, the look of anticipation in her eyes has me acting on instinct.

"You know, there is one thing I think I need some coaching on."

"Okay . . ."

Leaning in toward her ear, I line my lips up to her neck and say, "I'm not sure how I fare in the dirty talk department."

Her breath hitches. "Oh. Uh . . ."

"I mean, you know when you're making out and things start to escalate? I think I need your expertise on how to make the girl know just how crazy she's making me."

Her hands grip my shoulders to steady herself just as mine find her hips, pulling her into me so she can feel just how much this idea is turning me on.

And in case you were wondering, I don't need help in this department. I mean, sure, I've said some crazy shit in the heat of the moment, but nothing that kills the mood. And all of the romance novels I've been reading have definitely been helping with my dirty talk vocabulary.

Perhaps it's time to test it on the woman I want to know how to turn on more than anything.

"Well, uh . . . we could work on that."

"Are you sure you're okay with me testing this out on you?"

"Yeah, I can handle it."

I lean back to meet her eyes again, and I notice her pupils are dilated, her breathing shallow. Seems she likes this idea just as much as I do.

"Good."

That's all I say before smashing my lips to hers, stealing her breath. Pressing our bodies together—hers up against the side of her house and mine up against hers—I mold my body along her curves, pushing my erection into her stomach and placing my thigh between her legs, which she instantly starts to grind against.

"Fuck, Ariel. You're so fucking sexy. You've been driving me crazy all night."

"Uh-huh," she moans as her hips keep moving, undulating along my leg. My cock strains against my pants, but my lips keep up their assault on hers, making sure her body temperature—along with her need—rises just as high as mine.

"That's it, Ariel. Let your pussy do the talking. Show me what she wants. Show me how badly you want to come."

"God, I need it," she pants. "Jeffrey . . ."

I reach between us, flicking the button open on her shorts before dipping my finger along her soft skin. "Is this okay?"

She nods rapidly. "Yes."

"I want to make you feel good, sweetheart."

"Yes, Jeffrey. Please . . ."

I bite her bottom lip, dragging it out from her mouth slowly. "God, my name sounds good coming off your lips."

She takes my hand and shoves it down her shorts, behind her underwear, and I find her drenched as I run my finger through her slit. "Holy fuck."

She pulls my mouth back to hers, kissing me wildly as I begin to play with her clit, tease her opening, and shallowly dip my fingers inside of her, making her moan and pant against my mouth.

This woman is going wild in my arms. She's showing me a side of her I've been dying to discover. How she went from the woman who used to give me a perfected glare of annoyance to the one who is now writhing against my hand and attacking my tongue with her own I don't know, but right now, Ariel is proving that she's as desperate for this release as I am to give it to her.

And I hope it's because it's *me* and not just because we're friends or we're crossing the lines of fake dating that have pretty much evaporated at this point, as far as I'm concerned.

Friends don't normally give each other orgasms, do they?

"Right there," she whispers, breaking our kiss and leaning her forehead against my chest as I bury my face into her neck, teasing her skin there. "Don't stop."

"I hadn't planned on it. Are you gonna come for me, Ariel?"

She nods, digging her nails into my arms. "Yes. I'm there . . . I'm . . ."

A whimper escapes her lips before she covers her own mouth, breathing and screaming against her hand. She's shaking in my grip and grinding on my fingers working her over, drawing out every last tremor from her body. When she finally starts to calm, she removes her hand, leans her head against the house, and takes in deep breaths, her eyes closed as I watch her come down from her high.

Meanwhile, my cock feels like it could hammer nails, but that's all right. I can take care of myself later. This was about her. This was about showing her how good we are together, how much I want to make her feel desirable and wanted and how comfortable she is with me to let go the way she did.

When her eyes pop open, they lock on mine, darkened by the lack of light but also the obvious lust coursing through her body. "That was . . ."

When I can tell she's not going to say anything else, I ask, "How was that?"

"Uh, yeah. I think you're good."

I pull my hand from her shorts, bringing my fingers to my mouth to suck her arousal off of them. And fuck, does she taste good.

Her eyes widen as she tracks my movements. "Jeffrey," she gasps.

"Hmm," I mumble around my fingers, popping them from my mouth and then smirking down at her, trailing one of my soaked fingers along her jaw. "Fuck, you're addictive."

"You have to stop," she whispers.

"Stop what?" I challenge.

"The dirty talk. I think . . . I think you made your point."

"Aw, babe. I could go on all night. Remember, I read scripts of this all the time. I've got a dirty vocabulary for days."

The corner of her mouth tips up. "Then I guess your extracurricular studies have paid off for you because that was—"

I capture her lips before she can say anything else. Twirling my tongue with hers for a few more minutes, I allow myself to indulge in her for a little while longer.

"Okay. The date is now a ten," she says when we part.

I fist-pump the air. "Fuck yeah!"

"Shhhh." She presses a finger to my mouth, grinning up at me. "Don't wake up the neighbors."

"Sorry to break it to you, but you may have already done that. Even behind your hand, you were a little loud, babe."

She swats my chest, forcing me to back away from her. And my body is instantly cold, missing her warmth. But my cock is still hard as a rock and hot against my leg.

Her eyes drift down to the outline of my erection in my pants, widening when she takes me in. I'm not a huge guy, but I have enough to work with and make a woman feel good. And Ariel gives me the confidence to know that I can definitely please her more when the time comes.

And it will. It has to. No one could deny the chemistry here.

"I'd better go inside." She gestures to the house behind her. "Thank you for a perfect date."

"You're welcome. And hey, we made it out without any bodily harm," I say, lifting my hand for a high five, which she reciprocates with a roll of her eyes.

"We did." With one more press of her lips to mine, she opens the door. "Goodnight, Jeffrey."

"Goodnight, Ariel. Sweet dreams, babe."

Blushing, she shuts the door after her, leaving me alone on the porch with a steel erection, shallow breathing, and *hope*—hope that I'm so damn close to making this woman mine.

Chapter 12

Jeffrey

"Holy shit," Kellan says, adjusting himself in his chair. He just finished reading a spicy scene out loud, and from the looks of it, it did its job turning him on.

See? This is one reason women can read these books in public with a straight face and be horny as fuck from it because no one would know. Their body isn't going to outwardly display their arousal—except for maybe hard nipples, but that happens spontaneously, anyway—and they can go on their merry way with perhaps just some damp underwear. It doesn't work the same way for guys. Now all of us know that Kellan has a boner. But he's not the only one.

I reach down and flip my cock up under the waistband of my

shorts. Learned that trick as a teenager, taming the beast by strapping him in. Works every time.

"Yeah, that was a hot one." Hayden puts his book down and then stares across the group. It's our monthly book club meeting, and this week, we're reading a book by Regina Emerson, who just so happens to be Grant's mom. Grant is married to Noelle, who is best friends with Charlotte, Damien's wife. In fact, two more women make up their close-knit group of friends, Amelia and Penelope, and the four of them never steer us wrong with racy romance novel recommendations, particularly Noelle, because she is a literary agent and actually represents Grant's mother.

It's a tangled web of connections that I can explain another time. In fact, I think someone wrote down all of their stories somewhere.

"The next time I see Grant, I'm going to give him shit about the sex scenes his mom writes," Hayden continues.

"Be careful. You know he gets testy about that."

Hayden smirks. "I know. That's what makes it fun. I even got Maddox in on it at one point, but Penelope put a stop to it."

Penelope is married to Maddox Taylor, the quarterback of the Los Angeles Bolts football team, the same team that Hayden plays on.

"All right, you two. Let's finish this chapter." Kellan gathers our attention again. "Popcorn . . . John."

It was my idea to instill the "popcorn reading" tactic during book club like we did back in grade school, and fuck if it doesn't make the night more fun.

"Fuck you," John replies as we all snicker. "You all just like to hear me say the word 'cock.'"

He's right. You see, John is from Texas, so when he says "cock," his accent comes out thick, and it sounds more like *caulk*. It's the funniest fucking thing.

"Come on now, John. You're holding up everyone's reading experience," Hayden suggests, shoving him from the side.

We all barely keep it together as John finishes the aftermath of the sex scene, and much to everyone's dismay, he only says cock twice. But as we go to clean up and put our chairs back at the tables in Valor Books, curiosity gets the best of me. I take the legal pad out of my book bag, grab a pen, and start doodling, trying to envision the scene we just read.

"Uh, Jeffrey. What are you doing?" Hayden hovers over my shoulder, watching me work.

"Something about that position just doesn't make sense in my brain." Sticking my tongue out, I flip back to the page in the book and try to depict where everyone's arms and legs go.

"And you think drawing it out will help you understand?"

"Well, Joey from *Friends* did it, so how hard could it be?"

Shaking his head at me, he grabs my pen and completes the picture. "Like this. She's laying over the arm of the couch but on her back. That's what allows her to suck him off like that and for him to play with her."

"Ah, I see. Thank you."

"Glad I could be of service."

"Say . . . have you talked to your brother lately?" I ask Hayden as I shove my legal pad and book back in my bag.

"Actually, yeah. He asked me if I would consider being a guest on the talk show."

"And what did you say?"

"Well, normally I would have no problem doing something like that, especially because it's the off-season. But he wants me to do something kind of crazy on camera."

"Like what?"

"Well, you know how my sister, Hazel, does photography?" I nod. "She does these stranger photo shoots where the people are blindfolded and take pictures together but don't reveal themselves to each other until they're done. They want to do one live on air to boost their ratings and Hazel's business."

"That sounds fucking crazy—and also kinda hot."

"I know."

"So what's the holdup?"

Hayden rubs the back of his neck. "I don't know."

"It's not like you to overthink things. You're Hayden Palomar. You grab life by the balls and see where it takes you. I say do it. What's the worst that could happen? You meet a hot chick and end up taking her home that night?"

His face softens, and then his signature grin comes out to play. "Fuck, you're right. It might be kind of fun."

"Exactly."

Kellan and John come over after the other two guys leave, interrupting our conversation. "Hey, Jeffrey? I forgot to ask you.

Whatever happened with that woman who crashed our last meeting?"

"You mean Ariel?" Instantly, my mind veers to her, even though I was already visualizing putting her in the exact position drawn out on my paper just moments ago. At this rate, the woman doesn't ever leave my mind for very long.

"Oh, he's dating her," Hayden replies for me.

"Fake dating her . . . but also, really dating her?" I say, tapping my chin in thought. The definition of what we're doing is getting rather fuzzy.

"Wait . . . what?" John asks.

"I took a page out of the fake-dating book we read a while back. I told her I needed help with dating after she turned me down when I asked her out. But really, I just wanted a chance to get to know her. She's actually my sister's assistant on her show, so it worked out well that we crossed paths a few times. But now . . ."

"Oh, shit. I know that look," John says, pointing a finger at me. "It's not fake anymore, is it?"

"Not for me, and I'm beginning to think it's not for her, either."

"It always works out that way with that trope." Kellan nods his head slowly. "Everyone thinks they can keep feelings out of it, but someone always catches them."

"Well, I've had them from the beginning, but she was reluctant to date, so I did what I had to do."

Hayden slaps me on the shoulder. "Now, you just need to hope this all doesn't blow up in your face."

Grimacing, I say, "I hope it doesn't, but there's always that risk.

I knew that from the beginning. But the thing is, I still went through with it. However, the more time we spend together and the more we talk, my gut tells me her feelings have grown, too. There's no way that this is only one-sided given the way she's been acting with me."

"Well, I wish you luck, brother." John slaps my back. "You deserve to find your person. I've always wondered how you're still single."

"Gee, thanks."

"I mean it, though, Jeff. You have a lot to offer a woman. You just need to find the right one. It changes everything." John is married, and Kellan is on his way there. The other men in the group are also all attached. Besides Hayden, I'm the only single one, and I may have vented a time or two about how I kept striking out with the ladies.

"Well, I think I finally found her, guys. Now, I just need to figure out how to keep her."

∼

"Finally." I finish typing a few words on my computer and then click save, leaning back in my chair while placing my hands behind my head, admiring my work.

I just completed the presentation for the Pampers account and can now breathe a little easier.

My workload will be lighter come Friday, my relationship with Ariel is progressing smoothly, and I have a lunch reservation in thirty minutes with Damien at one of our favorite local spots that I'm desperately looking forward to.

But I've got something on my mind that I haven't quite figured out, and my sister is the one I really want to talk to about it, particularly because it will require Ariel to take a day off of work.

"Hello?" Joselyn answers on the first ring.

"Well, hello, sis. How's it going?"

"Oh, well . . . things have been better." I hear a door slam in the background and then the sound of heels on hardwood.

Suddenly, I'm sitting up taller in my chair. "What's wrong?"

Sighing, she groans. "Oh, Jeffrey. My house . . . it's a mess!"

"What happened?"

"I'm not sure, but it seems like a pipe or hose that's connected to my dishwasher broke. I started it before I left for work yesterday morning, and when I returned home, the bottom floor of my entire house was covered in several inches of water."

"Shit. Is the damage . . ."

"Oh, it's bad. I can't stay here until the repairs are done. I've already called the insurance company, and they've sent over a contractor, but—"

"So where are you gonna stay? I mean, shit—you know you can always stay with me, Jos."

"If you lived closer, I would totally take you up on that offer, Jeffrey. But a two-hour drive to work every day, probably longer with traffic, doesn't seem feasible. Plus, I'm sure you'll want alone time with Ariel here soon. She seems pretty jovial lately. I take it things are going well?"

That little piece of information makes me smile, but then I remember why I called Jos in the first place—to talk to her about Ariel and my idea. But after learning what she's been through in the past twenty-four hours, I don't want to bother her with my menial problems.

"Yeah, they are." Sighing, I run my hand through my hair, more focused on Joselyn's situation right now than my own. "Well, where will you stay? In a hotel?"

"No, uh . . . a friend offered me a place to stay."

"Okay. Well, I feel a little better that you won't be alone. But are you sure?"

"Yes, Jeffrey. It sucks, but that's what insurance is for. And at least I get new flooring out of this mess." I hear a voice over the line, and then Joselyn says, "Look, I've got to go. Did you need something still?"

"Oh, no. I'm good. Just wanted to check in with you."

"Well, things are a shit show at the moment, but I'm managing. I love you. Talk soon!" And then the line goes dead.

"You ready for lunch?" Damien walks through my office door just as I set my phone down on my desk, deep in contemplation. I'm not sure I feel comfortable with my sister being out of a living situation, even if she's staying with a friend. But at this point, there's not much else I can do for her except what I offered.

Looking up at my friend, I try to turn my frown upside down. "Yeah, I'm starving."

Damien stares at me, his eyebrows pinched together. "Everything okay?"

"I guess. I was just talking to Jos. Her house flooded."

His brows instantly rise. "Oh, shit. Has she called her insurance?"

"Yeah, she's handling it. But I wish I could help her more, you know?"

"I understand. You two are close. But if she says she has it handled, she does. Nothing irritates Charlotte more than when I question her." He holds up his hands. "So I've learned to just trust what she says and step in when it feels necessary."

Standing from my desk, I grab my jacket off the chair and slip my arms inside. "Fair point. Although, I was hoping to pick her brain about Ariel when we were talking, but her situation trumped mine."

"Well, maybe I can help? You know I've had my own success with the ladies."

Grinning at my friend, I say, "Let's not revisit your life before Charlotte. She's made you a better man, my friend. And hell, she's taught you more about women than you ever understood before her."

He chuckles. "Yeah, you're right." Staring off at the side of my office, he says, "God. It seems like so long ago. Remember how idiotic we were? How out of touch we were with everything women go through? Hell, I can still remember the night you showed up at my apartment with three hundred dollars' worth of period supplies."

"You're never gonna let me live that down, are you?"

Clutching his stomach, he says through his laughter, "Fuck no. That night lives rent free in my head now."

"At least we know more about periods than the average man."

"True. So, what's going on with Ariel that you can't talk to me about?"

"It's not that I can't. It's that I feel like I need a woman's perspective. I have an idea, but I need to know if it's too much. She's got trust issues, man. I can feel it, and I need a woman to help guide me is all."

Damien buttons his jacket as we head for the elevator. "Well, if I can't help you, I just so happen to know a group of women who will tell you the truth, even if it isn't what you want to hear. And they happen to have a brunch date this Sunday."

~

Walking into Frankie's Diner with sweaty palms isn't how I thought I'd be spending my Sunday morning. But when Damien suggested I ask the women in our group of friends for advice, I knew he was right.

Charlotte, Penelope, Amelia, and Noelle have been meeting for brunch since they were in college, where they met and sealed their everlasting bond with tattoos. And when Damien started fake dating Charlotte, he actually crashed one of their brunches to confront her after they hooked up for the first time. The rest is history, really, and thanks to their love story, I have now been adopted into the Ladies Who Brunch as an honorary member. Plus, I fucking love breakfast food.

Thankfully, they overlooked my penis because I always added a dash of pizzaz and spontaneity to the meeting. But it's been a long time since I've crashed their ritual, so I think I'm long overdue. And I know they can help me.

And talk about a strong group of women. Their men are some of my favorite people, too, but honestly, I fell hard for these girls. I'm obviously closest with Charlotte since she's connected to Damien and I see him more often, but Amelia is a sex and marriage therapist who is always a go-to person for relationship advice, Noelle is a firm believer in love since she publishes romance novels for a living, and Penelope has so much sass and balls-to-the-wall attitude, which serves her well in her public relations position for the Los Angeles Bolts—that, and you can always count on her for good ol' honest advice.

I admire them, felt honored to be a part of each one of their love stories—however small my role was—and now, I hope they get to be a part of mine.

"Well, well . . . looks like the honorary fifth member of the Ladies Who Brunch is here," Penelope declares, raising her champagne glass in the air as our eyes meet while I walk toward their usual table.

"Jeffrey!" Noelle exclaims as she rises from her seat, nearly falling over but catching herself at the last minute. Seems maybe she's already had too much champagne. "What are you doing here?"

I intercept her hug and then help her back into her seat, grabbing a chair from a nearby table and straddling it as I sit down. "You ladies have room for one more this morning?"

Penelope contemplates her decision for a moment too long, but then she puts me out of my misery with a knowing grin. "Yeah, I think we can handle that."

Amelia reaches for my hand, her smile warm and inviting as usual. I always feel comfortable around her, even when she's reading the shit out of me. As a therapist, she almost has a sixth sense of what's going on in your mind, but she never makes you feel like you can't have a conversation with her without her psychoanalyzing you—even though I do need to spill my guts a bit today. "Talk to us, Jeffrey. It's been a while since we've seen you. What have you been up to?"

"Well, I come to you lovely ladies today in need of some advice." Sheepishly, I say, "I met a woman."

"Oh! I like where this is going already." Charlotte gets comfortable in her chair, sipping her mimosa. "Damien mentioned something to me already, but hearing it from the horse's mouth is different."

Penelope fills a champagne flute, topping it off with a splash of orange juice, and hands it to me across the table. I eagerly accept it, take a sip, and smack my lips in approval. "Damn. Mimosas are so underrated. I forgot how good they are."

"We didn't. Why we drink them every chance we get." Penelope smirks. "Sadly, our little brunch dates don't happen weekly like they used to. Monthly, if we're lucky now, but that just means we take advantage and make up for a month's worth of lost mimosas when we congregate."

Noelle hiccups. "Yeah, I think Grant might have to come pick me up because I definitely shouldn't be driving." The girls laugh, and the sound makes me instantly smile. I fucking love drunk Noelle. "So tell us about your woman, Jeffrey," she purrs, trying to sound seductive, but it does not come off that way.

"Uh, okay. Well, her name is Ariel—"

"Like the Little Mermaid?" Noelle practically shrieks.

"Shhh," Charlotte admonishes, placing her finger over Noelle's lips. "You need to reel it in, girlfriend, or I'm cutting you off."

Noelle mimics zipping her lips and throwing away the key, giggling behind her hand.

Winking at her, I continue. "Anyway, yes. Her name is Ariel, and she's my sister's assistant on her talk show. When I went to surprise Joselyn for her birthday, I took one look at her and something shifted in me. But of course I made a Little Mermaid joke the moment I met her, too, which was a surefire way to piss her off. You know me, though—I charmed my way around it."

The girls exchange glances.

"Charmed her *how*, exactly?" Amelia asks.

"I, uh . . ." Scratching my head, I say, "Well, you see, I had bird poop on my shirt when we met . . ."

"Of course you did," Charlotte says through a laugh.

". . . so she gave me a shirt to change into. And I caught the way she checked me out. Let's just say there was a moment of appreciation, and I used it to my advantage."

Penelope bounces her eyebrows. "Have you been working on your fitness, Jeffrey?"

I flex a bicep. "You know it, Pen."

She clinks her glass against mine. "Good for you."

"Continue before your ego gets too big," Charlotte mutters, taking another drink as she stares at me.

"Well, long story short, I asked her out, and she turned me down. But then I got an idea."

"Oh, that's a dangerous thought," Noelle pipes up.

I point a finger at her. "Hey! You weren't supposed to talk anymore!"

Her hands come up by her face. "Sorry. I may have said it, but you know I wasn't the only one thinking it."

"True story," Penelope adds. "What was your idea, Jeff?"

Clearing my throat, I realize I'm a little nervous about what their reaction might be. But it's too late to go back in time now. What's done is done. I just need to make sure that I make Ariel mine for real.

"Well, she used that dreaded phrase: 'I think we're better off as friends.'"

Penelope winces. "Ouch."

"Yeah. And damn, you guys, I'm tired of hearing it. I know I'm goofy and say pretty much anything on my mind—"

"It's one of your endearing qualities, I think," Amelia interjects.

"Thanks, babe." I clink my glass with hers. "But I have a lot to offer someone, and I really wanted to get to know her. So . . . I asked her to be my dating coach so I could spend time with her and hopefully get her to see that we could be good together if she just gave me a chance."

"Oh, Jeffrey," Charlotte groans, tossing back the rest of her drink. She places her glass on the table, sighing. "Did you not learn anything from me and Damien?"

"I did! I saw how it worked out for you two and thought, why can't that happen to me? You were actually my inspiration."

"But Damien and I both knew it was fake. And with you and Ariel—wait." Her brows draw together. "Does she know that this was all a ruse for you to actually date her?"

"Uh, not exactly . . ."

Charlotte slaps her forehead, but I turn my eyes to the other women.

"Well, has she taught you anything?" Penelope chimes in.

"Why does that matter?" Charlotte fires back.

"Because if he's learned something, then it wasn't for nothing. I mean, no offense, Jeffrey, but we are very familiar with your obstacles with females."

"I know, and believe me, the past month hasn't been smooth sailing at all. But things have definitely shifted, and now I'm kind of at a crossroads."

"Well, how far have you gotten with her?" Charlotte asks, changing her tune slightly.

Noelle raises her glass, almost spilling her drink all over the table. Charlotte grabs it from her hand as she pouts but quickly turns her attention back to me. "Yes. I think we need to know everything that has happened thus far between you two to accurately assess the situation and/or damage."

I agree, so I spend the next several minutes relaying our dates and everything that's happened since. The girls listen raptly, asking questions, laughing at my expense when I talk about my bloody nose, saluting me when I tell them about Ariel's allergic reaction and how I handled it, and even cheering me on when I tell them about the physical developments that have happened as well.

"Oh, using the dirty talk lesson . . . fucking brilliant." Penelope smacks the table.

"I thought so myself." Grinning, I refill my glass with the perfect mimosa mixture.

"You know, I always knew you'd be a skillful lover," Amelia says.

Turning to my right to face her, I tilt my head. "Really? Why do you say that?"

"Because you listen to women," she replies. "You may not be the alpha man and stand out in that way—"

"I hope there's a *but* behind that statement."

She laughs. "There is. *But* . . . you understand women on a level most men don't. You observe, listen, and value friendship and connection. Most men only think with their dicks and then try to make up for it later."

I hold a finger up. "Uh, I want to be very clear. My dick has definitely been a factor in this situation."

"Oh, I don't doubt it," Amelia replies. "But your patience and dedication to developing a relationship first are what give you an edge."

"I hope so."

"So then . . . if things are going well, your intentions aside, what did you want our advice on?" Noelle asks.

Running a hand through my hair, I set my glass on the table in front of me. "I need to seal the deal. I need her to know that I'm all in, that even though this started out fake for her, it was real for me the entire time, and she's who I want."

Noelle fans her face. "Ugh. That's so romantic. Book boyfriend material for sure."

Grinning, I continue. "I want to take her away for the weekend, but I'm not sure that she'll go for it. It's kind of hard to justify an overnight stay when our situation isn't real, at least in her mind."

"Where do you want to take her?" Charlotte chimes in.

"Well, Ariel has this obsession with fountains. There's a hotel in Rancho Bernardo that has an entire trail of them with the history behind each one. The resort also has a top-of-the-line spa, and Ariel made a comment that she's never been to one, so I wanted to surprise her with that."

Amelia pats me on the shoulder. "See? You listen. I think she'll love that."

"I do, too. But how do I convince her that it's a good idea as part of my coaching? I mean, an overnight stay might suggest certain expectations of what could happen . . ."

"You don't convince her. You tell her how you feel," Penelope declares confidently, crossing her arms over her chest.

"What?"

"You want her, right?" I nod. "So tell her that. Tell her that over the past month you've realized that you're not interested in anyone else, that spending time with her has shown you that she's the one you want. And based on how you say she's responded to your dates—which doesn't sound like much coaching has been going on, anyway—I think she's feeling the same way."

"I think so, too."

"So be honest with her. Get your girl, Jeff. Stop playing around and go after her. Channel your inner alpha." She waggles her eyebrows. "It's really that simple. Trust me, don't waste time being apprehensive, contemplating everything that could go wrong. Just trust your gut."

Inhaling deeply, I sit up taller in my chair. "You know what? You're right."

Charlotte clears her throat. "I have to agree with Penelope. A hardcore declaration of your feelings will definitely help seal the deal."

"I'm just afraid of scaring her. She's definitely skittish about relationships."

Charlotte grabs my forearm. "That's why honesty will help. Tell her you guys can go as slow or as fast as she wants, but you only want her. Women have a hard time resisting that."

"My gut is telling me she's the one. I just don't want to mess it up."

"I have a good feeling about this one, too, Jeffrey," Amelia adds, turning my attention toward her again. "And I think it's time for you to get your happily ever after."

"Fuck, I hope so." Then I grab my glass that's been magically refilled and raise it in the air. The girls follow suit before I declare, "To finding love . . . thank you for helping me get there."

"And to mimosas!" Noelle exclaims.

We clink our glasses together as we laugh, and then I gracefully leave brunch, letting them enjoy the last bit of their meal without a penis involved, but grateful nonetheless. With renewed confidence, I return home, texting Ariel when I get there, eager to set my plan in motion.

Chapter 13

Ariel

"Don't fall asleep on me."

The vibrations of Jeffrey's voice through his chest have me lifting my head to meet his eyes. We're currently sitting on the couch in my living room watching *The Great British Baking Show* on Netflix.

"I'm not."

"You sure? I thought I heard you snoring just now."

My mouth drops open. "I don't snore!"

"Hmm. That's still up for debate."

Smacking his chest, he catches my hand and spins me so I'm now staring up at him, cradled in his arms.

"I mean, it's been a long week, but I wasn't sleeping. I swear. The show is gaining traction, so we've been working hard to come up with new ideas to keep ratings high. The studio execs are putting pressure on us to keep up the momentum."

He brushes hair from my face, trailing his finger down my cheek. "I know. Joselyn told me. She's excited, but it seems there's still some animosity between her and Hunter."

I divert my eyes from his. "They're, uh . . . working through it."

His eyes narrow on me when I look back at him. "What does that mean?"

"Nothing."

"I don't believe you. I think there's something you're not telling me." His hands move to my ribs where he begins to tickle me, and I scream. "Maybe I just need to tickle it out of you. How does that sound?"

I'm grateful that my mom's not here this evening. I don't have to worry about being loud and waking her up. It's after eight on a Friday night, and Jeffrey just arrived an hour ago after driving down to San Diego right after work. He insisted on seeing me tonight, and I was not about to deny myself the pleasure, either.

He offered to take me to dinner, but after the week I had, I really just wanted to stay in and relax. And my mother had plans for the evening, so it worked out perfectly for us to have some privacy.

In fact, my mother is staying with her new boyfriend, Vincent, tonight. The man she's been talking to online for months is now a permanent fixture in her life, and the change it's made in her has inspired me to make my own. All week, I couldn't wait to see

Jeffrey, felt giddy every time I opened up a text from him, and caught myself daydreaming about his lips and being in his arms more than I care to admit.

But right now, I'm on the verge of karate chopping him if I can just get my hands free.

"Jeffrey! Oh my God! Stop!" I wheeze, on the verge of not being able to breathe. "You know . . . I'm . . . ticklish!"

He moves his head to the side. "Oh, I remember. But I am not about to take another foot to the nose, woman." His fingers dig harder into my ribs, and then he moves to my armpits. "Now, tell me what you know!"

"Never!" Laughing, he tortures me for a few more seconds before abruptly stopping. Fighting for oxygen, I stare up at him. "Truce?"

With an arch of his brow, he says, "Nope. I just thought of another way I could get some information out of you. A different type of torture that I'm sure will work." His heated gaze makes my entire body break out in goosebumps. And when his lips curl into a mischievous smile, I can't decide if I should just tell him what I know or keep waiting to see what he's going to do next.

I decide on the latter.

"Take off your shorts." His command comes out low and gravely, igniting lust in my veins.

"Jeffrey . . ."

"We can do this the easy way or the hard way, Ariel." Leaning closer but still hovering over me as I lay across his lap, he whispers, "You know you want me to touch you, sweetheart. So humor me. Let me have my way with you."

Swallowing down the lump in my throat, I reach down and unbutton my shorts while keeping my eyes locked on him. "Is this supposed to make me want to tell you things?"

"We'll see, won't we?" He reaches for the remote and pauses the show. "All I know is I can't eat you out while people are talking about baked goods on the TV."

"Wait, what?"

"That's right, babe. We may have been watching people make dessert . . . but I'm about to make you mine."

He spins me around and then deposits me on the cushions of the couch so I'm lying down. I watch him stand up and then lift me so my torso is on the cushions, but from the waist down, I'm draped over the arm of the couch. And then his hands find the waistband of my shorts and pull the fabric down my legs, exposing me to him except for the blue cotton thong that I'm wearing.

"God, you're perfect." Staring down at me, he trails his fingers up and down my legs.

On a shaky breath, I say, "This evening just took a turn I wasn't expecting."

"Ariel, I've been thinking about this all week. I want to be a gentleman, and don't worry—I haven't forgotten what we were just talking about. But I'm about to fucking devour you, and it's gonna make all of my wildest dreams come true." Damn. He's sure well versed in the dirty talk. Those romance novels *are* doing him good. "Is that okay?"

"Yes," I say breathlessly, practically panting at the prospect of feeling his tongue on me.

"Thank fuck." Jeffrey bends down and kisses me, stroking his tongue against mine in a slow rhythm, building me up even higher. When his lips leave mine, I notice his eyes have grown darker and more intense, especially as he moves to the other side of the couch's arm, taking a knee in front of my legs. Gently, he presses my legs open as my entire body comes alive with anticipation. And then he drags his nose up my soaked underwear, inhaling deeply.

"So sexy. How long have you been wet like this, Ariel?"

"All week," I answer honestly because it's true. I've thought of the orgasm he gave me last week every night before bed and pleasured myself to the memory.

"And have you been thinking about me? Is that what has you soaked?"

"Yes . . ."

"Music to my fucking ears," he says and then presses the flat of his tongue against my slit. I shiver from the sensation, feeling him close but not enough. The fabric is in the way, and as if I told him telepathically, he hooks his thumbs in the strings on my hips and pulls my thong down my legs, licking his lips when he sees me bare for the first time.

"Fucking heaven. Goddamn." Running his thumb through my lips, parting me so he can see everything, I stare up at the ceiling, focusing on breathing as every sensation below my waist becomes heightened.

"Look at me, Ariel." I push up on my elbows so I can see his eyes and the top of his head between my legs. My body is trembling from nerves and anticipation, but Jeffrey's gaze has me most on edge. Even though he's about to go down on me, I've never felt more safe, more content.

And it's because of him.

With our eyes locked, he drags his tongue up my slit, landing on my clit and flicking it ever so lightly. His touch is heavenly, smooth but accurate, the perfect amount of pressure.

"You like that?" he mumbles against me, sucking my clit between his lips this time.

"So much."

"Good." His finger begins to toy with my entrance as his other hand pushes my thighs further apart. Moving in slow circles, he rubs around my entrance before teasing me with just the tip of his finger while continuing to suck on my clit.

"Fuck," I moan, gripping my knees, holding myself open to him, granting him better access while hoping that he fills me up completely soon. My release is building at an alarming rate.

But then nothing.

"What? Why'd you stop?"

"Did you miss the part where I said this was torture?"

"Oh God, Jeffrey," I groan throwing my head back. "You're a dick."

An evil laugh escapes his lips. "I guess that puts me in the same category as Hunter now, doesn't it?" I glare at him. "Speaking of Hunter, what's going on with him and my sister?"

"God, you're infuriating. You're seriously using me to get

information about your sister and her coworker?"

"Yup. Although, I'll make you a deal. If I let you come, you promise to tell me what you know. But you can't go back on your word once you get what you want . . . agreed?"

I contemplate his terms for less than a second. "Okay."

"Damn. You're that desperate for my tongue, babe?"

I grab the back of his head and shove it toward my pussy again. "Yes. Now finish what you started."

Chuckling against me, Jeffrey gets back to work, sliding his tongue all over my sensitive flesh, licking and sucking on my clit as he works two fingers inside of me. And when the simultaneous movements all come together, the edge of bliss comes into focus.

"Right there, Jeffrey. Oh God, please, don't stop."

He groans as he stays focused on moving his fingers in and out of me, curling them just right while flicking my clit with his tongue. And a few seconds later, I'm shattering, breaking apart as he lets me ride out my release.

When I collapse on the couch, giving my back a break, I feel him pounce on top of me, scooting us up the couch so we can both fit as he nestles between my legs. And then he captures my mouth with his own, the taste of me still on his tongue.

"Goddamn, woman," he mumbles between kisses. "You're sexy without question, but watching you come with my head in between your legs?" He shakes his head. "That was one of those visions I don't think I'll ever forget."

"Jeffrey . . ."

"Do you feel this, Ariel?" he asks, lifting his head so we can see each other.

"Feel what?" I reply nervously. I'm still naked from the waist down, but the look in his eyes has me more anxious for what he's about to say.

"*This* feels right, doesn't it? Being together? Spending time together? Touching each other? I can't remember the last time I craved someone like I crave you. The more time we spend together, the more time I just want to spend with *you*. I haven't thought about doing anything with another woman the entire time we've been hanging out. So . . . let's just make it official. I want us to date exclusively, honestly, so we both know what's happening here."

I bite my bottom lip. "I'm scared, Jeffrey. I like you . . . more than I thought was possible."

"I knew you'd find me irresistible at some point," he teases.

I smile, but it's hesitant. "And I feel the same way . . . being your coach this entire time never felt that way. It felt like I was the woman you were interested in."

He moves to speak and then stops himself. After a few moments, he lands on, "From the first date, I realized you intrigued me, and suddenly I just wanted to get to know *you,* not anyone else."

"So are we really doing this?"

"That's what I want, Ariel. I want to date you for real because it's felt real for me since the beginning. The question is: Do you want that, too?"

Panic rises in my chest, but then I remember how I felt all week

—and it's exactly what he just said. I already knew I was falling for him, and the past few weeks have shown me the man he really is. I'm still scared shitless, but I want to take the risk, even though I'm terrified of the fall.

"I've felt it, too," I whisper, watching his lips spread into a smile that lights up the entire room.

"I fucking knew it."

"Don't get too cocky there, mister. But yes, Jeffrey. I get it. The thought of you dating some other woman hasn't settled well with me since the night I ended up in the hospital."

"God, babe." He presses his lips to mine. "That night scared me. I don't think I've ever felt that way about a woman. I hated how helpless I felt when I couldn't protect you."

My heart just continues to melt for him with every word he speaks.

"So can we make this official and cut the bullshit? I want to date you, Ariel. I want you to be mine."

I feel like I'm about to jump out of a plane and I'm giving Jeffrey control of the parachute. The trust I'm giving him is something I've been fighting to keep locked in a box for years. But I want to give him that gift. I think, for the first time, a hope is attached to that gift, something I haven't ever felt with any other man. Kind of like throwing a coin in a fountain, I'm going to put that optimism out into the universe and just pray for once that it comes back tenfold.

"Okay."

"Okay?" he asks.

"Yes. I'm yours, Jeffrey."

"Damn right, you are," he says before stealing my breath with a kiss again. Grinding against each other, we make out like a couple of horny teenagers, his cock grinding against me with only his shorts separating us. "Fuck, I can't get enough of you."

"I feel the same." Reaching down between us, I pop the button on his shorts, yank down his zipper, and reach into his briefs, pulling his cock out and stroking him softly.

"Fuck, Ariel. Stroke me, baby."

"You feel so good," I mumble against his mouth, and then the head of his dick hits my clit, and we both hiss. "Do that again."

Jeffrey makes shallow thrusts, hitting that bundle of nerves, building me up again even though I just came a few minutes ago.

"I'm not gonna last, babe. Can you come with me?" he asks while pushing my shirt up higher, exposing my stomach.

"Uh-huh."

He keeps sliding across my slit, never entering me but stroking along all of the sensitive flesh between my legs that has me fighting off my release until I feel Jeffrey tense above me. And then my orgasm slams into me as well.

"Shit." He spills his release on my stomach, continuing to thrust so the waves of my orgasm crest and subside in time with his.

Lying there, a mess between us, he says, "You're so perfect." With a soft kiss to my lips, he rises from the couch, heading to the bathroom to get a towel to clean us up.

Once we're dressed again and settled back on the couch, I stare up at him, my chin resting on his shoulder. "We're really doing this?"

"Yeah, babe. We are. In fact, I have another question I want to ask you."

"Um, you might have filled your quota for the night."

Huffing out a laugh, he says, "I hope not. But this is important. I wanna take you somewhere."

"Okay..."

"Alone. For the weekend. Just the two of us. What do you say?"

"Are you sure? Doesn't that seem kind of fast?" I ask, more for myself than him. Jeffrey's confidence is unwavering, but mine is still fresh. Agreeing to date him is a huge step for me. I don't know if I can handle more so quickly.

"Not for me. I've had this idea for weeks, but now I feel like it makes more sense to go as a real couple than a fake one—or whatever the hell we were doing."

"Wow. Well..."

"Trust me, Ariel." He lifts my hand and kisses the top of it. "You'll love it. It will be the perfect way to start our relationship—romance, food, and only one bed." He growls out the last part, heating up my body again.

"Well, when you put it that way... I guess that doesn't sound so bad."

"Fuck, yes." He kisses me urgently and then says, "I promise, Ariel. You won't regret giving me a chance."

God, let's hope he's right about that.

Chapter 14

Jeffrey

"Wait . . . you're telling me that my sister is living with Hunter right now?" Casting a look over at her while I'm driving, I watch Ariel bob her head.

"Yes, but you can't confront her about it."

"Why not? We tell each other everything, and she hasn't told me shit." I run my hand through my hair as I try to focus on the road.

"It's only been for the past two weeks—"

"Two weeks!" I practically shriek. "Jesus Christ. So that's the friend who is letting her stay with them while her house is being fixed? *Hunter?* The man whose murder she was planning a month and a half ago?"

Ariel laughs under her breath. "I guess so. Joselyn just told me last Friday before I left work and you and I saw each other that night. Apparently, Hunter insisted she stay with him since he lives so close to the studios. Plus, they could ride into work together. I mean, it kind of made sense."

"I need to talk to Hayden about this," I say, reaching for my dash to connect my Bluetooth, panic rising in my body. When I get like this, it has to go somewhere. Seems like Hayden is going to get to talk me down off the ledge this time.

But Ariel stops me, placing her hand on my forearm. "No, Jeffrey. This isn't your concern. Joselyn and Hunter are adults, and they can figure this out. I'm sure your sister will come to you when she's ready and if she needs you. She's a big girl. I'm sure she knows what she's doing."

Ariel's touch and calm voice helps bring me down faster than I'm used to. But I guess that's what happens when you're with the right person—they sense what you need before you can.

Sighing, I relent. "Fine."

"Thank you. Plus, I don't want to ruin our weekend with you upset about them." She runs her fingernails up the back of my neck, digging into the hair there.

And fuck, it feels amazing. I can't wait to feel her nails all over my body at one point. "You're right. But something just doesn't add up, Ariel."

"That's not your problem to solve. You should focus more on telling me where exactly it is that you're taking me and what we're going to do when we get there."

Reaching for her hand to interlock our fingers, I focus back on the road. "That would ruin the surprise. And just so you know, now that I'm your boyfriend, get used to them. I want you to feel cherished and wanted always." I kiss the top of her hand as she bites her lip.

"I'd say you're already off to a good start."

After last weekend when I laid my heart on the line, I could instantly feel Ariel change with me. Part of me is nervous about how quickly she was willing to give this a shot since, in the beginning, she was so adamant about not dating. But now, all I want is to prove to her that her taking the risk with me is worth the reward.

As I watch her relax, hopefully opening up to me a bit more, I know showing her the thoughtfulness and care that she deserves is only going to build a strong foundation for our relationship.

I'm not gonna lie. I'm hoping there's some sex in there, too. However, Ariel is calling the shots with that. I told her so this week when we spoke each night on the phone, anticipating this trip. I don't want her to feel pressured to move too fast, even though we've already done things to each other. But we can still play along those lines until she's ready to give me that part of her.

And when she is, I'll be ready. The Costco-sized box of condoms in my suitcase says that much. I grew up in the Boy Scouts, so I know the motto: Always be prepared.

As we get closer to the resort, hills of green stretch out in front of us. We pass by residential neighborhoods and other hotels before finally turning a corner and pulling into the circle driveway of the Rancho Bernardo Inn Golf Resort and Spa, located about twenty minutes north of San Diego. I couldn't care less about the golf course here, but the spa and fountain tour are something I know Ariel will love.

"We're here," I announce as I shift the car into park in front of the lobby.

"This place is gorgeous," Ariel says, staring out the window at the building. The main lobby of the hotel is detailed in various shades of brown stone, almost giving it a castle sort of feel. Vines crawl up the sides of the structure, and plants line the sidewalk and driveway. And just in front of the main door is a fountain—the first of many.

"I can't wait to show you the rest." I step from the car and move to her side, helping her out. A bellhop comes over and loads our suitcases from the trunk onto a cart and then follows us inside. Once we check in, the attendant behind the counter hands me a mesh bag filled with leaves, coins, and flower petals.

"For the fountain tour," she says.

"Perfect. Thank you."

"A fountain tour?" Ariel whispers, her hand in mine, as we follow the bellhop to our room on the other side of the resort.

"Yes. I can't wait to show it to you. It's the main reason I wanted to bring you here."

We pass through lush gardens filled with blooms of all different colors, the pool with private cabanas you can rent, the spa with appointments already booked for us tomorrow, and several fountains on our way to our room. Ariel's curiosity pulls her toward them, but I don't want to visit them out of order. It's an experience, and we need to do it right.

After I tip the bellhop and shut the door behind him, I find Ariel staring out the window of our room, a view of a private garden in front of us.

"Jeffrey," she breathes, her voice full of awe.

"The spa is one of the best in the county," I say, wanting to tell her more about why we're here. "When you said you'd never done that for yourself, I knew I had to take you here. And the fountains . . . we can walk around later and see them all."

Before I can finish, she rushes toward me, leaping into my arms and smashing her lips to mine. I let her kiss me with every ounce of passion pouring out of her. I let her climb up my torso and bury her hands in my hair. And after I take a few steps toward the bed, I let her fall backward, pulling me down on top of her.

Breathless and beyond turned on, I pull away from her. "By that reaction, I'm guessing you like your surprise?"

With tears in her eyes, she looks up at me. "This is the most thoughtful thing anyone has ever done for me. I'm . . . I'm speechless."

"Well, if you kiss me like that when you have no words, I shall find other ways to make that happen again."

Smiling, she cups the sides of my face. "I'm serious, Jeffrey. This is incredible. Thank you."

I kiss the tip of her nose. "Anything for you, babe. I told you —I'm in this. Every word you've ever said to me, I took them all to heart. And . . ." Pushing myself from the bed, I move over to my suitcase and unzip the pocket, pulling out the plastic bag of coins I brought. "Here are some of the lucky coins I've found over the years. I want you to make all the wishes you can think of."

She stands and walks over to me. "One of mine has already come true."

"And what was it?"

"That you would prove to me that not all men can't be trusted. That there is somebody out there who could make me want to be vulnerable again. And you surpassed my expectations, Jeffrey. You've made me"—she takes in a shaky breath—"really fucking happy for the first time in a long time."

I pull her into my chest. "I feel the same fucking way, Ariel. See? Some wishes do come true. Now, let's try to make some more."

~

"I don't know about this one." Staring up at the top of it, my mind only veers to one place, a place that freaks me out any time I see this fruit now.

Ariel's brows draw together. "Why? It's gorgeous."

"The top of it looks like a pineapple."

"And that's a problem because . . . ?"

"You don't know what pineapples represent?" I turn to her, feeling the need to educate her on a piece of knowledge I learned years ago when Damien was fake dating Charlotte.

"Uh . . . it's a fruit, Jeffrey. What is it supposed to mean?"

Leaning close to her ear, I say, "Pineapples are a symbol for swingers, babe. Displaying them means you're open to swapping partners."

"Oh my God." She playfully shoves me. "You're not serious."

I put my hand in the air. "Scout's honor, I swear! Do you want me to call Charlotte and have her explain it to you?"

She rolls her eyes and looks back down at the pamphlet. "No. I think I'm good."

"You don't believe me?" I will die on this hill before I let Ariel think I'm wrong. And I know, it's not about being right all the time in a relationship. Compromise is more important. But I'll be damned if my woman thinks I don't know what I'm talking about when it comes to this.

"No, I do, it's just—"

"What does the pamphlet say?" I point to the trifold cardstock in Ariel's hands. We're on the first fountain of the tour, the one that was right in front of the main building where we checked in. And I really wanted this to be a monumental experience for her, but this freaking pineapple on the top of this fountain is making my anxiety flare.

"The Fountain of Hospitality was created by combining two antique pieces into one design. Toss a pineapple mint leaf into the water as a symbol of hospitality."

I snort. "Funny how it represents hospitality when a pineapple literally welcomes people into your home to bone your wife."

Ariel smacks my arm. "Oh my God, Jeffrey."

I simply shrug. "Keep reading."

She clears her throat, shoots me a glare, and then moves her eyes back to the paper. "The pineapple has been a symbol of hospitality in America since the 1600s . . ."

"So people have been swinging since back then?" I exclaim. "Good to know."

Rolling her eyes, she stuffs the pamphlet in her purse and takes the two mint leaves from the mesh bag for the tour. "Let's just make our wish, shall we?"

I wave my hand toward the fountain. "After you." Ariel tosses hers in, and then I follow suit. "So what did you wish for?" I ask her.

"For you to stop freaking out about damn pineapples," she mutters and then takes off toward the next fountain.

I can't help but laugh, catching up to her and kissing her until she's smiling again. Luckily, the rest of the tour goes by smoothly—no odd social symbols that spark my anxiety in sight. Only watching Ariel learn about the history of each fountain, watching her make wish after wish using some of my coins—which makes my heart thump fucking hard—and we finish at the Santiago Lawn Fountain where we toss in the final pebble for good luck.

The lawn is tucked into a quiet corner of the resort with a view of another resort in the distance and beautiful plants all around us.

"That was amazing," she finally says to me, breaking the silence we were just sitting comfortably in. The sun is setting in the distance, and we have reservations for dinner in about an hour. The cuisine served in the restaurants here is five star. I can't wait to stuff my face. And I even made sure there were no hazelnuts in the vicinity before I booked our stay.

"I'm glad you liked it."

"I did. Like I said, I don't think anyone has ever put that much thought into something for me before."

I wrap my arm around her shoulder and pull her closer to me, tipping her chin up with my other hand. "I think about you all the time, Ariel. I haven't stopped since I met you. I don't want you to ever doubt that."

I can see her swallow, and then her face contorts in thought. "I'm trying. It's just . . . hard. The last man I was with . . . he said all the right things, too, Jeffrey. And then he devastated me, cheated on me the entire time I was with him. I never saw it. Or . . ." She turns her eyes away from me, staring off into the distance. "Maybe I just didn't want to see it."

"I'm so sorry that you've been hurt like that," I say, instead of asking for the guy's name so I can look him up and beat the shit out of him. No wonder this woman was so reluctant to date after that. "But I promise, I would never do that to you."

Her eyes find mine again. "I know that. I know that *now*, at least. That's why I trust you. It's why I'm taking this leap of faith and giving you my heart because I know you would never lie to me."

My chest twinges from her words as I realize that perhaps that statement is not as true as I've been telling myself it is.

I mean . . . have I lied to Ariel?

When I asked her out and she turned me down, I came up with the idea for her to coach me, hoping it would make her fall for me.

And it worked.

But does Ariel need to know that? Do I need to tell her that I never needed her help? That I just wanted her? Or that I was so damn tired of being stuck in the friend zone with a woman that I finally made a slightly questionable decision to get me out of it?

Or does it even matter anymore since we're together and happy and everything worked out the way it was supposed to?

"Every man in my life has always lied," she says, bring me back to the moment and twisting the knife a little deeper in my heart. "Even my own father."

"How?" I ask, wanting to keep her talking. This is the most she's ever opened up to me, and that says something. She's trusting me, and yet, part of me is now questioning whether I deserve it or not. I remember her changing the subject about him early on in our relationship, and she hasn't brought it up since.

But she's bringing it up now because you're together, and that says a lot about how she feels about you.

"He had another family, Jeffrey. When you asked me about him on our second date, I . . . I didn't want to talk about it because it still hurts. And things were different with us. But now, I want you to know." She grabs my hand, staring down at where our fingers are joined. "He had children with another woman and built a family with her behind me and my mother's backs for years. When we found out, I felt like my entire life had been a lie. It's made me question men ever since, but I don't want to project that onto you."

"Fuck, Ariel. I'm so sorry."

"Thank you, but it's not your fault. And it's not mine, either—at least, I'm working on believing that. But I want you to know why I'm hesitant about relationships, why I might freak out from time to time. I know I already agreed to this and told you I have feelings for you, too." She takes a deep breath and blows it out. "And that's true. I guess I'm just asking you to be patient with me, and now you know why."

I kiss her temple. "I appreciate that. And I promise to be patient and help you see that it's okay to trust me. I'm not going anywhere. I'm not your dad, and I'm not your ex. I'm the man who's going to be everything you've ever wanted, baby. I promise." Stroking the side of her face, I watch her smile transform, lighting up the bubble around us. We're outside, and the sun is setting, but Ariel is shining brighter than the sky in the distance.

"I wondered if I'd ever feel this way about someone, but I guess I was just waiting on you." She leans forward and presses her lips to mine, and nothing has ever felt more right. Even in the back of my mind, I debate whether I should tell the entire truth to her, but I don't know that it would do any good at this point.

It's time to just move forward. Be together. Be happy. And be way more than just friends.

∽

"That food was incredible." Ariel rubs her stomach as we walk under lighted archways covered in plants on the way back to our room.

"It was. And that wine?"

"Yes. We need to buy a bottle before we leave on Sunday."

The resort serves wine from local wineries all over southern California. During dinner, Ariel and I sampled several and found a few new favorites. Perhaps a wine tour will be our next weekend getaway now that I know she enjoys it like I do.

"We will. Tomorrow, though, is all about relaxation and pampering, babe."

She lets out a high-pitched squeal. "I'm so excited! And also kind of nervous."

"Why nervous?"

"I don't know. The idea of strangers rubbing me down . . ."

"Oh. Well, I'm sure they've seen all kinds of bodies, and probably nothing phases them anymore. You don't have any weird-shaped moles or third nipples or anything, right?"

She smacks my arm. "No."

"Just asking. You know, I've seen most of you unclothed but not all of you."

She stops right in front of our door, resting her back against it. "Well, would you like to change that?" The heat in her eyes instantly makes my blood rush south.

"Fuck, babe. You know I do, but we don't have to do anything you're not ready for." I smooth her hair away from her face. "I told you that."

"I know. But I'm dying here, Jeffrey." She yanks me forward by my shirt, rubbing the tip of her nose along mine. "I want you so much."

"Fuck, I want you, too, Ariel."

"Then take me."

Trembling from nerves and anticipation, I draw in a deep breath and then smash my lips to her mouth, moaning once we make contact. I'm aware we're outside of our room in the hall and anyone could walk by at any moment, but I don't care. The way this woman makes me feel doesn't make me want to hesitate when I have the chance to show her just exactly what she does to me.

I fumble for my pocket, pulling out my keycard to unlock the door while our mouths stay connected, tongues lashing and lips sliding against each other's until the sound of the lock engaging has me pulling away from her to get us safely inside.

But once we are, everything moves fast.

Ariel pushes my shirt up my torso as I reach back to rip it over my head. And then she smooths her palms down my chest.

"I can't believe I get to touch you like this now."

"I saw you checking me out that day in Joselyn's dressing room." I fan my arms out to the sides. "And now it's all yours, baby."

She giggles and then presses her lips to my pec, moving her soft, pillowy lips across my skin. She flicks her tongue against my nipple, making me groan, and then reaches for the button on my slacks as she continues to explore my chest.

I bury my hands in her blonde locks as she pushes my pants down, leaving me in nothing but my boxer briefs once I kick off my shoes and socks. My eyes are closed as I try to focus solely on her touch, but then I think about how long I've wanted her like this. I don't want to miss a second of it, so I open them again to watch her.

Pulling her head up, I find her mouth once more, reaching to unzip the back of her dress and help her step out of it. And fuck me, she's not wearing a bra.

"Damn, baby. Your breasts are perfect."

She licks her lips. "They're sensitive, too."

Jesus, I think I might come faster than I did when I was a teenager.

But then she hooks her thumbs in the sides of her thong and bends over to drag it down her legs, stepping out of it and leaving her completely naked before me for the first time.

My dick physically reacts to the sight, dripping pre-cum from the tip while twitching erratically.

"Are you trying to kill me, woman?"

"No. I'm trying to show you what's yours, Jeffrey." She takes a few steps toward me, pushing her hand through my hair. "I want you to make me yours. Please."

I desperately search my brain for an image that will help me fight to keep control. And hey, it works. Each man has their own trick. Ask them, and they just might tell you. "Your wish is my command."

"I *have* wished for this," she whispers against my lips, taking my bottom one between her teeth and pulling gently.

"Me, too, baby. Me, too."

After kissing her breathless, I force myself to release her mouth. I hurry over to my suitcase, grab a condom from my stash, and head back to the bed where Ariel is already lying, waiting for me.

I push down my briefs, freeing my cock, and quickly crawl over her, place the condom to the side, and bury my head in her neck, sucking and nibbling on her skin. Then I trail a path over her collarbone and down to her nipples, eager to suck on them.

"God, yes, just like that," she moans as I gently flick her nipple, reaching down between her legs to play with her as I do.

"Is that good?" I rub her clit with my thumb and drag my tongue in circles around her peak simultaneously.

"Yes . . . more, please."

Maneuvering my hand, I push two fingers inside her and find her clit again with my thumb. I keep playing with her nipples, switching to the other side after a moment to share the love. And the sounds she makes, how she yanks on my hair, the way she calls out my name as she comes all over my hand has me digging through the files of nonsexual images again.

Thank God my mind is holding me at bay.

"Fuck, you're so sexy when you come." I find her mouth again as I feel her body relax after her release. "But we're not done yet."

"Oh, I know we're not." She reaches between us and wraps her hand around my cock, stroking me gently, squeezing hard as she reaches my tip.

"Okay, you need to stop, or this is going to be over way too soon."

Giggling, she reaches for the condom, rips it open, and rolls it down my length.

So. Fucking. Hot.

And then she positions me right at her entrance and bites on her bottom lip. "Fill me up, Jeffrey."

"Goddamn, woman. Where have you been?"

I push inside, working myself in even though she is soaked and ready. But I want her to feel good. I don't want to go too fast. But once I'm inside of her, I realize this may be over quickly anyway.

"Jesus, you feel incredible." I kiss her lips. "So fucking perfect."

"Make love to me, please."

Staring down into her eyes, I rest my forehead on hers and find a rhythm she seems to like. Her hips move up to find mine, and stars form behind my eyelids. I hook one arm behind her knee, forcing her leg up over my shoulder so I can slide in deeper, and the movement makes us both moan out loud.

Our touches are frantic but deliberate. Our kisses are messy but passionate. Our breathing is erratic yet intense.

Our connection is everything I thought it would be.

Sex has never been this magnetic, this life-changing. Being with Ariel is unlike any other sexual encounter I've ever had—because it fucking means something. It's the lens of my life coming into complete focus.

I don't want to say something too soon, but words I know for certain, down to my marrow, are on the tip of my tongue.

This woman is it for me.

She's the one I've been waiting for.

"Ariel, baby. I'm close."

Her nails dig into my shoulders as her breathing grows shallow. "Me, too. Touch me, please."

I follow her request, rubbing her clit softly—just the way she likes—and when I feel her contract around me, I stop holding back and chase my own release. My entire body tenses as I come, and intense euphoria spreads down my limbs while I cling to Ariel in my arms. Nothing else exists in this moment except the two of us. And I wouldn't have it any other way.

Collapsing on top of her, I shudder as she strokes her fingernails over my back. "Are you okay?"

"Just give me a minute," I mumble, waiting for the feeling in my legs to come back. Her laughter makes me pop my head up. "What's so funny?"

"Nothing. I'm just . . . happy," she says, her eyes glossed over.

So I give her a chaste kiss, hold back the words I really want to say, and land on, "I'm really fucking happy, too."

Chapter 15

Ariel

"Well, you look like you had an amazing weekend away," Joselyn teases me when I walk into her dressing room Monday morning. And then Jeffrey walks in right behind me.

After spending the day at the spa on Saturday and enjoying more food than we could stomach, we decided to stay one more night. Now, it's Monday morning, and Jeffrey drove me to work to drop me off before he heads back to Los Angeles.

We talked about how the distance between us would be a factor as our relationship progresses, but for now, we decided to just see how it goes. I'm just looking forward to the weekends when we will see each other. In fact, I'm headed up to LA this coming weekend to see his house and explore together.

And I can't fucking wait.

Even though things are going fast, I know in my heart that I'm already in love with him. I mean, how could I not be?

The man has proven his character time and again. He makes me feel beautiful, desired, and heard. I feel like we can be silly together, talk about anything, but also have amazing sex—which we took full advantage of for the rest of the weekend at the resort.

Sex with Jeffrey is like nothing I've ever felt. He's the perfect mix of gentle and rough. He asks what I like and if something feels good for me, a simple idea that I wish more men would consider. And his body is perfect for me—not too toned but strong enough that he could hold me up against a wall to fuck me. Of course, I'm barely over five feet, so picking me up isn't a problem, but Jeffrey acted like it was nothing.

And boy, did he deliver some stellar orgasms that made me pass out on more than one occasion.

So yes, my weekend was phenomenal. And my future with Jeffrey looks just as bright.

"Well, hello, sis," Jeffrey sings as he walks up behind me, wrapping his arm around my waist from the back, a move he became quite fond of this weekend, claiming me in public around other people. And I did not complain.

"Hello, brother," she snipes back at him. "I take it you two had a good time?"

Jeffrey nuzzles my ear, tickling me with his breath. "The best. Right, babe?"

"Yes," I say, trying to calm down my libido. We had sex one

more time before we left this morning, but I already want the man again.

"Gosh, you two are just too cute." Joselyn claps her hands, and that's when it hits me. She seems pretty lively and upbeat herself.

"How about your weekend? Anything fun happen?" Jeffrey asks, beating me to the punch. And I know he's trying to get her to crack about her and Hunter's living situation, but I'm not sure if she will just yet. I was actually going to wait until he left so I could grill her some more. But this time, I'm not telling Jeffrey shit. I felt bad telling him what I knew already, and I don't want Joselyn to feel like I'm betraying her trust.

"Oh, uh . . . it was . . . uneventful." Joselyn turns around and makes herself busy, avoiding our eyes.

"Really? Nothing happened with your new roommate?" Jeffrey prods.

Joselyn spins around to face us, her eyes wide. "No. Everything is fine."

Jeffrey narrows his eyes at her. "Really?"

I look at Joselyn just as her eyes meet mine, silently asking if I've told him too much. *Oh, fuck.*

"Ariel?" Melissa, one of the production assistants, pops her head into Joselyn's dressing room just in time, saving me from the inquisition I'm pretty sure was coming.

Jeffrey releases me from his arms as I walk over to her. "What's up?"

"I need your input on something. Do you have a minute?"

"Go ahead, babe," Jeffrey says. "I'll be right here until you get back, and then I've got to get on the road. I told Damien I would be back in the office by noon."

"Okay."

Following Melissa down the hall, I listen to the schedule they're trying to finalize for the next month and some of the issues they're running in to. I'm trying to focus on what she's saying, offering my two cents, but my mind is back in Joselyn's dressing room and the conversation happening between her and her brother right now.

After about thirty minutes of getting a few things done, I head back to the room I left earlier but stop outside when I hear the conversation on the other side of the door.

"I'm so fucking glad that I convinced her to coach me after she turned me down, Jos," Jeffrey said. "If I wouldn't have come up with the idea, we wouldn't be together right now. You know she wouldn't have given me a chance if she knew I wanted to date her from the start."

"I know, Jeffrey. I'm so happy for you. You two are perfect for each other. I saw it the first time you met."

The world around me starts to spin as I absorb what I just heard.

Jeffrey tricked me into dating him by asking for my help? And Joselyn knew about it?

That familiar feeling of having the rug ripped out from under my feet slams into me, and I nearly throw up my breakfast all over the floor. But I find an ounce of control over my anger, take a few deep breaths through my nose and out of my mouth, and debate what to do.

Unfortunately, I don't have time to contemplate if this is the right choice at the moment. I just react.

Swinging the door open, I draw their attention instantly.

"Hey, babe."

"I'm not your babe," I seethe, fighting off tears.

Jeffrey's brows pinch together. "What are you talking about?"

"You tricked me."

"I tricked you?"

"I heard you just now, Jeffrey. You convinced me to coach you so I would date you without me knowing." His eyes widen, and he takes a step toward me, but I hold up my palm, stopping him. "Don't. And you." I point a finger at Joselyn. "You knew about it."

Joselyn holds her hands up like I'm pointing a gun at both of them. And metaphorically, I feel like I am. "Ariel, just calm down, okay?"

Shaking my head, my lips start to tremble. "No. I can't." Glaring at Jeffrey, I say, "I trusted you. I trusted you not to hurt me."

"Ariel, you *can* trust me. I'm the same man I've always been."

"But you lied to me. You know how I feel about that."

"I didn't lie . . . I just—"

"Withholding the truth is the same fucking thing!" I shout. "I need . . ." I swipe under my eye as the first tear falls. "I need to go."

Jeffrey practically runs toward me this time. "Baby, please. Let's just talk about this."

"No. I need space. I need to get away from you right now. Both of you." Shooting a look at Joselyn—who looks just as upset as I do—I tell her, "I'm taking a personal day."

And then I run, ordering an Uber back to my house, thankful they show up within two minutes so Jeffrey can't chase after me. I climb into bed the second I get home, wondering how my life went from perfect to fucking shit so quickly.

And then I remember—this has happened before, and apparently, this is the way it's supposed to be for me forever.

∽

Jeffrey

"Jesus Christ!" I yank on my hair. "What just happened?"

My sister bites her thumb. "I'm so sorry, Jeffrey. She must have overheard us. I didn't think you could hear through that door so well."

"This is a disaster, Jos. I fucked up. I should have just talked to her about it earlier before I told her how I felt. We could have laughed about it and—"

"I really don't think it would have mattered. You know about her trust issues. It just sucks that she found out like this. And now she thinks we schemed behind her back."

"But did we?" I ask her. "I mean, you knew what I was doing."

"Yes, but she was also doing kind of the same thing."

My mouth drops open. "What?"

Joselyn motions for us to take a seat on her couch. "I'm only telling you this because I want you to have all of the information. I am not taking sides, nor do I think you're both innocent in this. But . . . Ariel and I had a conversation after she had that allergic reaction on your date."

"About?" My heart rate is through the roof right now as I wait for her to continue.

"She told me then that she could feel herself falling for you, but she wasn't sure if she wanted to. So after she told me a little about her past, I convinced her just to see how things went between you two and feel it out. And if, at the end of your arrangement, she knew she wanted to date you, then she should. I guess I was hoping that you two would eventually admit your feelings to each other, which you did, thank God. But I never imagined it would blow up like this."

I hang my head in my hands, my elbows resting on my knees. "Fuck, Jos. She was so scared, I don't blame her for waiting. And I don't regret my decision to ask for her help. But now?" I turn to face her again. "This can't all have been for nothing. I need to fix this."

"I'll try to help if I can."

"What do I do? Do I call her? Go to her house?"

She shakes her head. "No. I would give her some time."

"How long?"

"Well, let me see if she comes back to work tomorrow. If she's here, I'll let you know and then try to talk to her, get her to see both sides. Then we can go from there."

"I can't lose her, Jos." My voice cracks. "I love her. She's the one for me."

"I know, Jeff. You won't. This is just a little hiccup. You'll get past it."

"I sure fucking hope so."

Chapter 16

Ariel

"**G**ood morning." Joselyn greets me the second I walk through her door, but I don't look up. I spent the rest of Monday sulking and crying and then realized I was not about to waste any more tears on men.

Even if my heart is shattered into a million pieces and I just desperately want to go back to this weekend before everything fell apart—again.

"Here are the notes for the show today." I grab the paper from my clipboard and hand it to her.

"Ariel..."

"Is there anything else that you need from me?"

"Yes. I need to talk to you."

I finally lift my eyes to hers and see the remorse on her face. "I don't think that's a good idea."

"Well, I do, because I won't allow two people who are meant for each other to let the love of their life slip through their fingers." She folds her arms across her chest. "And especially because one of those people is my brother, I can't just let this go."

"Joselyn . . ."

"And Ariel? Let me remind you that you weren't exactly honest with my brother about your intentions while dating him, either." She arches a brow.

Fuck. I was hoping she wouldn't remember that, because I sure did. As soon as I got home and my mother asked me what was wrong, I rewound my entire relationship with Jeffrey, divulging how I made the decision to try him on for size during our arrangement. And that's when my mother so blatantly pointed out that neither of us was innocent then.

The reality of the situation put me in my place rather quickly, but I'm still fucking hurt.

Sighing, I stare at the ground. "I know. But it doesn't change anything, okay?"

"Please, just let me talk to you for a minute?" she pleads. "Let me say my piece, and then you can do with the information what you want."

Nodding, I head for the couch, and Joselyn meets me there. "Okay. Fine. Say what you need to say."

She grabs my hand, and I let her, fighting back tears that were already on the edge of falling this morning. "First of all, I'm sorry I lied to you."

"Thank you."

"I knew what my brother was doing, even when you confided in me, but I saw the spark between the two of you early on and was hoping that you both would discover it as well. Call me selfish, but I wanted to see my brother happy. And I knew you were scared, but I thought that giving him a chance may help you see that you didn't need to be afraid of him—that he is one of the good ones."

"He is."

"I'm glad you still feel that way, because that leads me to my next point. The only reason Jeffrey did what he did was because he wanted a chance to prove himself to you. It took a lot for him to take that risk. He's fought being the 'friend' with women his entire life. Women never saw him as a love interest. They saw him as the goofy side character who always provided a laugh. And he's good at that." She smiles. "But he also has a huge heart that was made to worship the right woman. And he chose *you*.

So, he may not have gone about it the right way, but when do men ever think things through?"

That makes me chuckle.

"Add on his verbal diarrhea, and you've got a man who just needs a little feminine direction."

"Ain't that the truth," I reply, feeling some of the weight lift off my chest as she keeps talking.

"But here's the important thing: It's not like he was pretending to be someone he's not. He was genuinely himself the entire time.

The goofball, the klutz, the man who can't control his mouth . . . that's all Jeffrey, every crazy ounce of him. And every bit of energy he expended was for *you*. Only you, Ariel. It's actually very romantic if you think about it. He knew you needed to take things slow. He showed you patience and kindness and everything he has to offer. He just wanted to offer it to you. And you had to let him do that. So yeah, he altered the truth behind wanting to spend time with you. But every moment between you was honest. Nothing about that was a lie."

Tears fall down my face as I think about our time together. And I know Joselyn's right, but it doesn't negate the fact that I feel blindsided. I swore I'd never let someone make me feel this way again.

"I just felt caught off guard," I say.

"I understand."

"And I overreacted in the moment. I know that Jeffrey wouldn't hurt me intentionally, but God, Jos . . . hearing it just brought me back to a very dark place."

She squeezes my hand. "I'm so sorry."

"But I do have feelings for your brother, crazy as it may be."

"You two can just be crazy together."

I huff out a laugh as I wipe away tears. "I want that, too."

She lets out a sigh of relief. "Thank God. He's going nuts, Ariel. You need to call him as soon as possible, okay? And just remember—you both got what you wanted out of this, so why does it matter how it started?"

Before I can argue with her further, there's a knock on the door.

"Come in!" Joselyn announces as Greg, one of the studio assistants, opens the door, holding a large arrangement of blue hydrangeas. They're stunning, and their fragrance instantly fills the room.

"There you are, Ariel. I went by your desk, but you weren't there, so I figured you'd be here." He walks toward me, setting the vase on the coffee table in front of the couch I'm still seated on. "These are for you."

"Really?" I lean forward to pluck the card from the stick holding it in place.

"Yup. Lucky girl." He winks. "Well, I've done my duty. Off to the next task."

"Thanks, Greg," I say as he salutes me and then leaves just as quickly as he came.

"Who are they from?" Joselyn asks, a knowing smirk on her lips.

I open the envelope and extract the card, reading as quickly as my eyes will allow.

Ariel,

Did you know that blue hydrangeas symbolize apology, regret, and forgiveness? I felt they were the perfect way to begin to show you that I feel the first two and hope that you can give me the chance to earn the third. I know you're upset right now, but I am pleading with you to not throw away how incredible we are together. My intentions were never malicious, I swear. All I wanted was the opportunity to get to know you because I knew once I did, I'd fall in love with you. Please, let me see you. Please, open your heart to the possibility that this is real.

With all my love,
Jeffrey

"Damn. I know that's my brother, but he's good."

I laugh and look at Joselyn, who's peering over my shoulder as I read the card.

"So, what are you gonna do?"

"I'll call him later."

"You're gonna make him sweat a little?"

I stand from the couch, grabbing my clipboard, and Joselyn follows my lead, straightening her dress. "Just a little. The man needs to know who he's dating."

She grins. "Damn. You're ruthless. I like it."

"I love him, Joselyn."

"I know you do. So get your man, Ariel. Don't let him get away. Prove to my brother that nice guys can still get the girl in the end."

Chapter 17

Jeffrey

I glance around the courtyard, waiting to see the petite spitfire of a woman walking toward me. But so far, there's been no sign of her.

It's fifteen minutes past the time we agreed to meet, and I left work as soon as I could to rush down here when she agreed to talk. I've endured forty-eight excruciating hours of agony, sweat, and an upset stomach that I can't control, and I won't be able to rest until I know things are okay with us.

Joselyn told me that she and Ariel spoke and it went well, so I'm hoping that's a good precursor to our conversation. However, I'm trying not to get my hopes up. Instead, I'm relying on the luck of every penny I've ever found heads up, sitting in the bag on the edge of this fountain. I mean, it can't hurt, right?

But then I see her—Ariel walking toward me wearing a blue sundress, her hair floating around her like an angel—and my world stops spinning for a minute. If this conversation doesn't go the way I want, I don't know how I'll bounce back from this.

How do you go on living when you know the person you're supposed to be with doesn't want you? I don't even want to think about it—even if I have to.

Frozen in place, I wait for her to arrive at the fountain—the same one we walked by the night she agreed to be my dating coach. And when she stands just a few inches in front of me, my knees nearly buckle.

I literally want to get on my knees and beg for her forgiveness, but that's a last resort. I'm not above begging, but I don't want to go there just yet and make a scene.

"Hi," she says, her voice soft and less assured than I imagined her sounding with the way she was just strutting over here.

"Hi."

"How are you?" She tucks a strand of her blonde hair behind her ear.

"I'm okay. Better now that you're here."

"Same. It's good to see you."

Her sentences are so short that it's making me nervous. But I don't want to react too soon.

"Same to you, babe. Wanna sit?" I gesture to the fountain behind us.

She bobs her head, and then we take a seat on either side of my bag of coins. "Are these yours?" she questions.

"Yeah. I figured I could use all the luck I could get."

Inhaling deeply, she stares down at her hands. "You don't need luck, Jeffrey. In fact, neither of us do."

Oh, fuck. I don't like the sound of that.

"What we need is honesty," she continues.

"I know," I interject desperately. "And Ariel, I'm so fucking sorry for misleading you."

"I know you are. And I'm sorry, too." Her eyes finally meet mine. "Because I kind of did the same thing."

"Jos told me what you were doing—trying me on for size, so to speak—and I get it. I understand why you did it. I know you were scared, and I don't blame you, given your past. But all I wanted was your future."

"I understand your decision, too. But something still doesn't sit well with me," she declares. "How can we build a relationship on a lie, Jeffrey? How can we move forward knowing how this started?"

I grab her hand, and she lets me. I wait for our gazes to connect before I keep speaking. "It wasn't a lie. Nothing I felt for you was a lie, Ariel. Were you lying about what you felt for me?"

"No."

"So then, we both got what we wanted. Don't you realize that I did what I did because I never wanted to date any other girl, never wanted to use what I learned from you with anyone else? That everything I did *with* you was always about *you*? I just needed you to see it, to see *me*, to give me a chance to be something other than your friend, Ariel. I wanted to be your prince, and you're the only girl I want to be my princess."

"God, you're so cheesy," she says, tears filling her eyes, but a smile graces her lips.

"You love it. And I love you." Her breath hitches. "I think I did from the first time you scowled at me and told me you weren't my sweetheart. So now I'm just asking for the chance to love you for real, forever . . . as long as you'll have me."

"I love you, too," she whispers. "I never thought I could love someone like I love you."

"Fuck. Come here, babe." I pull her into my arms, situating her on my lap before I find her mouth and kiss her so she can never doubt that what we have is real.

People continue to move around us, but our world freezes for a moment, where the only thing that matters is the two of us—and the fact that I finally found the woman I'm meant to be with.

When we come up for air, I rest my forehead on hers. "I'm so fucking sorry, and I promise, I'll never keep anything from you again."

"I promise that, too."

"So we're good?"

"Yeah, we're good."

"And you're my sweetheart again?"

She giggles. "I'm not your sweetheart."

"Yeah, I know." I move my lips just a millimeter from her ear and whisper, "You're my fucking everything."

THE END

Thank you so much for reading! If you enjoyed it, PLEASE take time to rate and review on Amazon and/or Goodreads! It truly means so much to an author and other readers.

If you would like a glimpse into Jeffrey and Ariel's future, find a FREE Bonus Epilogue here!

Thank you as always for reading my stories. It truly means so much! I am debating between releasing two different series next, so please sign-up for my newsletter here to be kept in the loop about future releases.

Acknowledgments

This book would not exist without my readers begging for it. I wasn't sure if I would write it, but when the idea popped into my head, I knew I needed to give it life. And boy, oh boy, am I glad I did.

Jeffrey reminds me a lot of my husband—goofy, funny, but has the best freaking heart. I'm telling you, ladies—marry the funny guy, the sweet guy. He's the one that will cherish you and make you feel like you have a true partner in life.

Don't forget to download the series epilogue to get a glimpse into the gang's future 10 years down the road! And don't worry—you'll get more of them in my future books too. And Jeffrey and Ariel's Bonus Epilogue and HEA will have you tearing up and so happy for the two of them. Make sure you read it here.

To my husband: Thank you for cheering me on and celebrating my success with me as I release each book. Thank you for understanding how much joy this hobby brings me. And thank you for being my real life book husband and giving me my own true love story to brag about.

To Keely: One of the best things that has come out of this

author journey is my friendship with you. I cherish our friendship so much! Thank you for always being there to chat and cheer me on. I love ya!

To Melissa: I am SO grateful for our working relationship. Your attention to detail and thoughtfulness shined throughout the process. Thank you for your dedication to my stories and I look forward to working together again.

To Melanie: As always, your expertise and friendship has made this author journey even more rewarding. I'm so grateful for our connection and honest discussions about this author gig. So thankful to have you in my corner.

And to my beta readers, ARC readers, and every reader (both old and new): Thank you for taking a chance on a self-published author. Thank you for sharing my books with others. Thank you for allowing me to share my creativity with people who love the romance genre as much as I do.

And thank you for supporting a wife and mom who found a hobby that she loves.

About the Author

Harlow James is a wife and mom who fell in love with romance novels, so she decided to write her own.

Her books are the perfect blend of emotional, addictive, and steamy romance. If you love stories with a guaranteed Happily Ever After, then Harlow is your new best friend.

When she's not writing, she can be found working her day job, reading every romance novel she can find time for, laughing with her husband and kids, watching re-runs of FRIENDS, and spending time cooking for her friends and family while drinking White Claws and Margaritas.

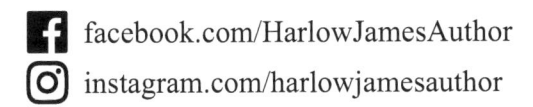

facebook.com/HarlowJamesAuthor
instagram.com/harlowjamesauthor

More Books by Harlow James

More Books by Harlow James

The Ladies Who Brunch

Never Say Never (Charlotte and Damien)

No One Else (Amelia and Ethan)

Now's The Time (Penelope and Maddox)

Not As Planned (Noelle and Grant)

Nice Guys Still Finish (Jeffrey and Ariel)

The California Billionaires Series

My Unexpected Serenity (Wes and Shayla)

My Unexpected Vow (Hayes and Waverly)

My Unexpected Family (Silas and Chloe)

The Emerson Falls Series

Tangled (Kane & Olivia)

Enticed (Cooper & Clara)

Captivated (Cash and Piper)

Revived (Luke and Rachel)

Devoted (Brooks and Jess)

Lost and Found in Copper Ridge

A holiday romance in which two people book a stay in a cabin for the same amount of time thanks to a serendipitous $5 bill.

One Look, A Baseball Romance Standalone (you can get this for FREE if you sign up for my newsletter)

Guilty as Charged

An intense opposites attract standalone that will melt your kindle. He's an ex-con construction worker. She's a lawyer looking for passion.

McKenzie's Turn to Fall

A holiday romance where a romance author falls for her neighborhood butcher.

Made in the USA
Columbia, SC
17 August 2024